MW01518646

MUSTANG WINGMAN

By

Thomas Willard

Approximately 36,000 words.

Contents

Introduction.. 1

Chapter 1 - Headquarters, USAAF Eighth Air Force: January -

May 1944 12

    High Wycombe 12

    Eighth Air Force: Formation and Early History 13

    Doolittle: Innovator.. 19

Chapter 2 — Wormingford Airfield: Return to Duty: April - July

1944.. 29

    First Salute 29

    Celebration 42

Chapter 3— Start of Second Tour: Mid-July 1944...................... 56

    Appeal 56

    Subterfuge 61

    Switch to Mustangs... 68

    55th Mustangs First Combat: Escort to Munich: 21 July 1944 71

Thomas Willard © 2021

Chapter 4 — Ramrod to Ruhland: 11 September 1944 74

Mission 623: Overview.. 74

Pre-Briefing Preparation 77

Mission Briefing 79

Ready Room.. 81

Battle of Ore Mountain: First Phase 84

Zoom-Climb Ram 86

Wingman Again 94

Emotional Shock... 104

Chapter 5 — Stanbridge Earls Revisited: 11-21 September 1944

.... 112

All-Hands.. 112

Dare Backfire 120

Duck Pond Purge 136

Back to Normal.. 146

Thomas Willard © 2021

Chapter 6 — Completing Second Tour-of-Duty: Mid-September 1944 to Mid-February 1945 154

Return to Duty... 154

Battle of the Bulge: 16 December 1944 to 25 January 1945 .. 158

End of Second Tour-of-Duty: Separation: Mid-February 1945

.... 163

Chapter 7 — Home: Mid-February to Mid-April 1945 168

Catatonic 168

Swampscott... 183

Luck of the Irish... 198

On the Mooring.. 210

INTRODUCTION

By late 1939, three months after declaring war on Germany and seven before the Battle of Britain, Great Britain's Air Ministry realized it was going to need more fighter aircraft than Britain alone could produce.

In 1938, the Air Ministry had licensed the Canadian Car and Foundry Company to build the Hawker Hurricane, powered by a Rolls-Royce Merlin 29 engine built by the Detroit automaker, Packard Motor Company, under license and redesigned by them for mass-production. But the Ministry knew that even with this added capacity, combined with the increase in Hurricane and Spitfire production at home, it was not going to be nearly enough.

In January 1940, the British Purchasing Commission was formed - headed by Sir Henry Self and based in New York City - to arrange the production and purchasing of armaments from North American manufacturers. The Commission reached out to US aircraft manufacturers to see if any were willing to produce British-designed fighters, but all were busy building their own designs. So, the Commission considered placing orders for existing US fighters, but none of the designs in production – the Lockheed P-38 Lightning, the Bell P-39 Airacobra, or the Curtiss P-40 Warhawk - met the British requirements. The closest was the P-40 Warhawk, but the manufacturer, Curtiss-Wright Corporation, was already operating at maximum capacity.

The only US aircraft manufacturer with excess capacity was North American Aviation (NAA), who's president, James H. Kindelberger, had approached the Commission in January 1940 about buying North American's new medium twin-engine bomber, the B-25 Mitchell.

North American was already providing the AT-6 Texan/ Harvard trainer to the British, who were impressed with the production quality and mass-production capabilities of the company. The Commission asked North American if it would be willing to build the P-40 under license from Curtiss for Britain.

North American countered that the P-40 Warhawk was based on a 1933 airframe design and offered they could design and produce a more advanced fighter - using the identical V-1710-39 Allison engine as the Warhawk - in the same time it would take to tool-up to manufacture the P-40.

At a meeting in early April 1940, North American's chief engineer, John L. Atwood, presented the preliminary design for a new fighter to the Commission, based on a concept developed by North American's chief designer, Edgar O. Schmued, who would later design another iconic fighter for North American, the F-86 Sabre jet.

After reviewing wind tunnel data for some of the features of the new design, the Commission agreed to the proposal, with one stipulation – that the prototype be ready 120 days after the start date. North American agreed to meet the prototype-delivery schedule, and the Commission issued a letter of intent on 10 April 1940 to begin development.

The legendary, second-generation WWII-era fighter design that North American produced was the P-51 Mustang, arguably the best piston-engine fighter of WWII.

The design was evolutionary rather than revolutionary, an amalgam combining the best-proven engine and aerodynamic technologies from the first-generation WWII-era fighters of both the US and Britain.

The keys to its success lay in: its low-drag, fuel-efficient airframe design; its eventual use of the highly reliable engine-driven, two-stage, two-speed supercharged Packard-built version of the Merlin 66 engine, the V-1650-7, which burned 130-octane fuel readily available in the UK and used on the Spitfire; and it's large internal and external fuel capacity, giving it approximately the same range as the P-38.

The plane was highly maneuverable, had a high roll rate, a maximum service ceiling of almost 42,000 feet, a maximum speed of 440 mph, and an operational range of 1650 miles with drop tanks.

It had a well-laid-out cockpit and was relatively easy to fly, greatly reducing the pilot-workload from that of the twin-engine P-38: a P-38 pilot could transition to the P-51 in an afternoon.

Low-drag was achieved by using: a new but evolutionary low-drag laminar-flow wing design, developed jointly by North American Aviation and the US National Advisory Committee for Aeronautics (NACA), with performance proven by full-scale wind tunnel tests; a conical-section lofted fuselage design; and a ram-air inlet scoop design located on the belly, again developed with the aid of full-scale wind tunnel tests, that provided air to the inlet of the engine, as well as the engine and supercharger-intercooler ethylene glycol coolant radiator, and the oil-cooling radiator.

The highly efficient scoop design, used on the Spitfire and Hurricane, took advantage of the Royal Aircraft Establishment

(RAE)-discovered Meredith effect: heated exhaust air from the radiators, run through a converging nozzle to form a jet, produced enough thrust to offset the aerodynamic drag of the scoop.

Armament was tuned for air-to-air combat and consisted of six wing-mounted .50 caliber AN/M2 Browning machine guns, aimed using the new K-14 gyroscopic gunsight, a US-produced version of the British-developed Mark II gunsight used on the Spitfire.

Visibility in the iconic, largest production model - the P-51D - was excellent with the change to a bubble canopy, like the one first used on the British Hawker Typhoon and Tempest.

Unlike the P-38, which was designed assuming low-volume production, the P-51 was designed from the outset for mass-production. The airframe fuselage was built in five main sections or subassemblies – the forward, center, and rear fuselage sections, and two wing half sections – with each section equipped with all the necessary internal electrical wiring and hydraulic tubing, then bolted together at final assembly.

Two production lines were eventually formed – one in Inglewood, California, and the other in Dallas, Texas – that had a combined average production rate of 350 planes a month, with 857 planes manufactured in a single month at peak production. The cost, in 1944 dollars, was $50,000 per plane, about half the cost of a P-38.

The first prototype airframe rolled out of the hangar on 9 September 1940, just 102 days after the contract was signed, an amazing engineering feat. It was fitted 15 days later with an Allison V-1750-39 engine and a 3-bladed propeller and first flew on 26 October 1940, reaching a speed of 382 mph, 25 mph faster than the P-40. It even outperformed the Spitfire at low altitudes.

The first shipment of P-51A/ Mustang Is was delivered to the Royal Air Force (RAF) in September 1941. The planes, equipped with Allison engines with single stage-single speed superchargers, lost power quickly above 15,000 feet, so they were restricted to ground-attack and tactical-reconnaissance roles only, but roles in which the Mustang Is excelled.

In April 1942, a Rolls-Royce test pilot, Ronald W. Harker, flew the Allison-powered Mustang I and was impressed by the plane's performance up to medium altitudes but was disappointed with its performance above that. He recommended switching to a Merlin 61 engine with a two-stage, two-speed supercharger and a four-bladed propeller and convinced a reluctant Rolls-Royce and the RAF to re-engine five Mustangs for a series of performance tests.

The Merlin-powered Mustang's performance, especially at altitude, was reported by Rolls-Royce's chief test pilot, Captain R.T. Shepherd, as "spectacular," with an increase in maximum speed to 432 mph. North American, who had been considering doing the same experiment with a Packard-built Merlin, quickly released two new models, the P-51B and C, equipped with the Packard V-1650-3 engine and a Hamilton Standard 11.2-foot diameter four-bladed propeller. Later, the D model, using a more powerful Packard V-1650-7 engine and with a bubble canopy, was released and became the iconic, most-produced model.

Quantities of long-range Mustang P-51Bs and Cs, with auxiliary 85-gallon fuselage fuel tanks, began to be delivered to the US Eighth Air Force in late December 1943. The Mustangs first started flying long-range bomber escort missions in February 1944, participating in Operation Argument (Big Week), and in March 1944, they joined bomber escort missions to Berlin, reducing the burden on the 55th and 20th Fighter Groups, still flying P-38Hs.

By the time the P-51D models began to arrive in May 1944, and probably as early as March 1944, the Commanding General of the US Eighth Air Force, Lieutenant General James H. Doolittle, came to the decision to switch all US Eighth Air Force fighter groups to P-51Ds as soon as possible. Due to the high-production rate of North American Aviation, by August 1944, all but one group had made the transition.

The impact of the US Eighth Air Force's change to Mustangs in the European Theater of Operation (ETO) cannot be overstated. Historians separate the US bombing campaign in Europe into two eras: pre-Mustang; and post-Mustang.

Prior to the introduction of the Mustangs, the US Eighth Air Force was losing badly to the German Luftwaffe, just hanging on, mostly due to the heroism and sacrifice of the P-38 pilots of the 55th and 20th Fighter Groups. After the introduction of the Mustangs and Operation Argument in February 1944, which was costly but finally broke the back of the Luftwaffe, the Allies quickly gained air supremacy, especially over France and Belgium, and by 4 April 1944, had swept the skies clear of German fighters along the English Channel, in time for the Normandy invasion on 6 June 1944.

A total of 15,588 Mustangs were built, and their WWII pilots are credited with 4,950 aerial kills, more than with any other Allied fighter.

No better testament exists to show the effectiveness of the P-51 than the US Eighth Air Force estimate of aerial-only kill ratios for the fighters that flew in the ETO during WWII: 2.6:1 for the P-38 Lightning; 7.5:1 for the P-47 Thunderbolt; and 10.7:1 for the Mustang.

Today, there are an estimated 174 airworthy Mustangs remaining, hopefully, more than enough to inspire at least two more generations of WWII aviation buffs, keeping the memory of the Mustang, the engineers who designed her, and the pilots that flew her into battle alive for several more decades.

CHAPTER 1 - HEADQUARTERS, USAAF EIGHTH AIR FORCE: JANUARY - MAY 1944

HIGH WYCOMBE

High Wycombe is a large market town in Buckinghamshire County, England, approximately 29 miles west-northwest of London. From May 1942 to July 1945, it was home to Headquarters, USAAF Eighth Air Force, officially known as Station High Wycombe (code name Pinetree). The headquarters was housed in a requisitioned girls' school, Wycombe Abbey School, which included a main house, the early-17th century

Loakes Manor, and was situated on 170 acres of woodland in the Chiltern Hills.

#

EIGHTH AIR FORCE: FORMATION AND EARLY HISTORY

On 28 January 1942, the Eighth Air Force was activated in the former National Guard Armory in downtown Savannah, Georgia. Its mission was first to destroy the German Luftwaffe and gain air supremacy over Europe; and second, to bomb and destroy Germany's war production - its factories, transportation systems, oil refineries, airfields, and fortifications throughout Nazi-controlled Europe.

In early February 1942, the Commander of the US Army Air Force, Lieutenant General Henry H. Arnold, sent one of his best generals and closest friends, Brigadier General Ira C. Eaker, to England to organize and command the Eighth Bomber Group. Another close friend, Major General Carl A. Spaatz, soon followed as Commander of the Eighth Air Force, comprised of the Eight Bomber Group and the Eighth Fighter Group.

Eaker worked closely with his RAF Bomber Command counterpart, Commander-in-Chief Arthur T. Harris, who had also just assumed his command. Eaker and Harris formed a close working relationship, and there was tremendous cooperation between them.

The Eighth Air Force greatly benefited from the RAF's earlier experience fighting the Germans and copied most of the RAF's organizational structure, even locating its headquarters near RAF Bomber Command in High Wycombe. The RAF eventually transferred control of over 100 airfields to the Eighth Air Force, effectively turning England into the world's largest aircraft carrier. Eaker and Harris had very different views, however, on how to wage the combined bombing campaign.

After suffering unsustainable losses in their attempt at strategic daylight bombing early in the war, the British were forced to adopt night area-bombing. Harris and the whole of the RAF high command, as well as the British Prime Minister, Winston Churchill, believed the Eighth Air Force would suffer the same fate and recommended combining the Eighth's forces with RAF Bomber Command's and joining their night area-bombing campaign under RAF command.

Eaker and the entire USAAF high command, as well as the US President, Franklin Roosevelt, believed strategic bombing would result in the quickest path to an Allied invasion of Europe and that the Eighth Air Force should remain independent but as closely coordinated with the RAF as possible.

By November 1942, the two commanders had agreed on the terms of their coordinated bombing effort. Both air forces would remain independent. The RAF's short-range fighters would provide air protection for the USAAF airfields in the UK, and RAF bombers would continue to area-bomb German targets, unescorted, at night. In parallel, the Eighth Air Force would bomb strategic German targets during the day, and their fighters would provide escort-protection for their bombers as far into Germany as possible. By bombing day and night, the two campaigns would complement each other, applying unrelenting pressure on the enemy.

The Eighth Air Force received its first group of bombers, the 97th Bomb Group, in July 1942. After a month of intensive training, the Eighth flew its first mission - with Eaker onboard the lead aircraft - bombing the marshaling yards at Rouen, France. The mission - in German-occupied territory and with the bombers escorted by British Spitfires the entire way to the target and back - met no flak and little Luftwaffe opposition. The Group suffered no losses, and the mission was judged a success.

Over the next year and a half, Eaker sent out over one hundred missions, not aimed, like the RAF area-bombing, at the civilian population of Germany, but at strategic targets selected to cripple the German war-machine.

But with increasing losses, Eaker soon realized the idea the bombers could defend themselves without fighter escorts was mistaken. The Germans had quickly developed the tactic of waiting for the short-range P-47 Thunderbolt fighters to reach their endurance limit at the German frontier and turn back before attacking the bombers, often resulting in an attrition, or loss rate, of over 20 percent.

In May of 1943, he began advocating for drop-tanks for his escort P-47 fighters and for additional fighter groups equipped with long-range P-38s and the new, long-range P-51 Mustangs. But Arnold and the other USAAF policy makers, who had other Theaters of Operation to supply, were reluctant to accept his recommendations.

Feeling increasing pressure from both at home and in the UK over the seemingly slow pace of operations and unnecessarily high casualties, Eaker launched the most daring offensive of the Eighth's air war to date, Operation Pointblank, sending over one thousand bombers into Germany, unescorted, during a one-week span in mid-October 1943.

Losses from the outset were high, but the week culminated with the disastrous second attack against the ball bearing factories in Schweinfurt, Germany, in which over sixty B-17s and six hundred crewmen were lost.

Despite the heavy losses and ineffective bombing results, the raid on Schweinfurt did help the war effort in one important way: it finally convinced Arnold, Spaatz, and the other policy makers of the urgent need for long-range fighters to escort the bombers deep into enemy territory. Without these fighters, particularly the new long-range P-51 Mustang, the bomber losses would grow to the point where they would be unsustainable.

In early December 1943, less than two months after the Schweinfurt raid, General Dwight D. Eisenhower was named Supreme Commander of the Allied Expeditionary Force (SHAEF), charged with overseeing Operation Overlord, the Allied invasion of Europe. Spaatz was named Commander of the US Strategic Air Forces in Europe (USSTAF), directing the US Eighth Air Force, based in England, and the US Fifteenth Air Force, based in Italy. Both the US Strategic Air Forces and the Royal Air Force Bomber Command, under Arthur Harris, reported directly to Eisenhower, while the US Ninth Air Force and the British 2nd Tactical Air Force indirectly reported to him through the Allied Expeditionary Air Force (AEAF), under the command of Trafford Leigh-Mallory.

One of Eisenhower's first acts as Supreme Commander was to name Lieutenant General James H. Doolittle - someone he'd work closely with during Operation Torch, the Allied invasion of North Africa - as commander of the Eighth Air Force. Eaker, who Arnold had expressed disappointment in after the Schweinfurt mission, was promoted-upward and reassigned as Commander-in-Chief of the newly-formed Mediterranean Allied Air Forces (MAAF), a position like Spaatz's in the Mediterranean Theater of Operations (MTO).

#

DOOLITTLE: INNOVATOR

Lieutenant General James H. Doolittle assumed command of the US Eighth Air Force on 6 January 1944. In hindsight, the timing of the change proved extremely fortuitous.

Eaker, with his exceptional organizational and political skills, had been just the right choice to build, from scratch, in close partnership with the British, the mightiest strategic bomber-force the world had ever seen. Now Doolittle, with his unique blend of engineering skill and decisive, innovative, aggressive, but not reckless, leadership style - honed by extraordinary combat experience – was the perfect choice to use the force most effectively.

Strategic bombing is most often credited for winning the war in Europe. But strategic bombing, and the Allied invasion of Europe, wouldn't have been possible without Allied air superiority.

It is now recognized by historians that pilot attrition won the battle for air supremacy in the European Theater of Operations through one-on-one aerial combat between fighter pilots, and Doolittle was the chief proponent of that strategy, starting from the day he took command of the Eighth Air Force.

Based on information received from German intercepts through Ultra, the Top-Secret decoding project at Benchley Park, Doolittle knew by January 1944, the Germans were already experiencing a pilot shortage and were scavenging their training instructors for pilots, sacrificing the quality of the training of new pilots.

Along with Spaatz, Doolittle devised the strategy of pressing the Luftwaffe fighter force at every opportunity.

The Germans were trying to conserve their fighter force until its strength could be restored, using it only to protect the most important targets or when they could attack with a large enough force to have a numerical advantage. So, Doolittle and Spaatz chose bombing targets of the greatest strategic importance to the Germans, like fighter aircraft manufacturing plants and oil refineries, and political significance, like Berlin and Nuremberg, that the enemy fighters had to defend. Without admitting it, maybe even to themselves, they used the Eighth Air Force's bombers as bait.

From May 1943, Eaker had advocated for long-range escort fighter protection for the bombers and requested the delivery of the newly-developed long-range P-38 and P-51 fighters to the Eight Air Force. Though his request was initially denied, after the disastrous Schweinfurt raid in October 1943, supplying the Eighth with long-range fighters was now a top priority.

Doolittle would soon benefit from Eaker's efforts, but it would take several months before the new fighters would arrive in quantity. In the meantime, he would have to make the most of what he had available.

The only fighters with a long enough range to escort the bombers deep into Germany to the strategic targets selected to bait the Luftwaffe were the long-range P-38s of the 55th and 20th Fighter Groups, but these planes were proving unreliable, with often half of the planes having to abort a mission due to engine failure.

Soon after taking command, Doolittle called on Captain Gordon P. Saville, one of the authors of the P-38's design specification and a P-38 test pilot - they also knew each other from their time as students at MIT - to help diagnose the problem.

Doolittle, an expert on high-octane fuel - he'd championed its development at Shell Oil and its adoption by the USAAF as its standard aviation fuel prior to the war – and Saville quickly concluded the engine problem was due to fuel detonation/ engine knocking and that that problem was due to low-octane fuel from fuel improperly blended in the UK: the British blended a lead-additive to standard 87-octane fuel to obtain the 130-octane aviation fuel needed for the US and RAF fighters.

Saville had just personally tested the P-38 in the US at 30,000 feet, using 150-octane fuel refined in the US, and had experienced no detonation at engine power/ manifold pressure settings of 2000 horsepower/ 75 inches of mercury, well above the placard rating of 1612 horsepower/ 64 inches of mercury for the P-38 using 130-octane fuel.

When Doolittle reported his findings, the British protested, pointing out that their Spitfires and Hurricanes were not experiencing engine failures using the same fuel. In fact, they were, but at a much lower frequency.

Doolittle now had a political as well as an engineering problem to solve. He knew the comparison between the fighters wasn't justified: both RAF fighters had a limited range, and so did little bomber escort duty. And most dogfights over England occurred below 24,000 feet, so the RAF fighters spent very little time at 30,000 feet, as opposed to the P-38s, which spent hours at high-elevation escorting the bombers, a role the planes had not been designed for.

He also knew the P-38s, due to a poor inlet-manifold design and from using a turbocharger versus a supercharger, were more prone to detonation, so they required a higher-octane fuel than the RAF fighters. The P-38s would be more sensitive to any decrease in octane-level due to improperly blended fuel.

So, Doolittle switched tactics. Rather than try and resolve the fuel-blending issue, he advocated for Eisenhower to increase the power rating of all Allied fighters in the ETO by 20% by using 150-octane fuel. But besides increasing the fighter performance across the board, this also eliminated the blending issue since 150-octane fuel was only available from US refineries.

Eisenhower approved the idea and made providing 150-octane fuel a high-priority – starting first with the P-38 squadrons - with the result that, by the D-Day invasion in June 1944, all Allied fighters in the ETO were using 150-octane fuel.

Doolittle then began denigrating the P-38, a plane he'd recently bemoaned the shortage of in his last command, once calling it "The sweetest flying plane in the sky." He now called the P-38 a second-rate fighter. His goal was to replace all Eighth Air Force first-generation P-38 and P-47 fighters with the new, second-generation P-51D to provide his pilots with the best fighter the Allies had, even if it meant unfairly diminishing the reputation of an outstanding fighter: he knew the P-38 was still in demand in the Pacific, where the US had total control over the fuel supply, so P-38 production wouldn't be reduced.

Having only a single fighter in the Eighth's inventory would greatly reduce logistic challenges. Also, moving to the P-51, with a single engine versus the P-38's twin-engines, would significantly reduce the workload of the line crews. And the easy to fly Mustangs greatly reduced the mental-demand on pilots, leaving them to concentrate on dogfighting, and had a much-improved gun sight.

But the change to the P-51 would also eliminate the possibility of any further politically-charged fuel issues since the P-51 used the same Merlin engine as the RAF fighters: he knew if there was ever a fuel issue, the British would be screaming louder than he ever could.

Eisenhower approved Doolittle's recommendation to replace all the Eighth's fighters with P-51s as soon as possible, and by August 1944, all but one of the Eighth's 15 fighter groups had converted to the new fighter.

Probably Doolittle's most significant contribution to the war effort, though, was his rescinding of the standing order that the fighters provide close-escort for the bombers, forcing them to fly at reduced speed, fighting on defense, eliminating the advantage of attack.

On 24 January 1944, Doolittle issued an order releasing the fighters from close-escort. He ordered the fighters to fly loose escort instead to what became known as "ultimate pursuit," to seek out enemy fighters up to 20 miles ahead of the bomber formation before they had time to form up or while they were still on the ground. He ordered them to aggressively attack enemy fighters on-sight. And to strafe airfields on return after their bomber-escort duty had ended.

This change in tactics was in line with Doolittle and Spaatz's strategic objectives of reducing the fighting effectiveness of the Luftwaffe's fighter force by destroying their fighters on the ground and in the air, crippling their fighter aircraft production, and killing as many of their pilots as possible.

It can be argued that the ultimate success of this strategy led to the Allies gaining air supremacy, first, over the Channel in time for the D-Day invasion, and then eventually, over all of Europe, culminating in the Allies winning not only the air battle over Europe but in their winning the war overall.

CHAPTER 2 — WORMINGFORD AIRFIELD: RETURN TO DUTY: APRIL - JULY 1944

FIRST SALUTE

Just as Matt and Jeff were getting settled into their new lodgings, their squadron's adjutant arrived requesting that, once they got themselves squared away, they report to their squadron leader, 23-year-old Captain James H. Hancock, the commanding officer of the 38th Fighter Squadron.

Soon after the adjutant left, Jeff noticed a change in Matt: he'd become quiet and seemed withdrawn. Jeff knew Matt well enough by now to know something was really bothering him, but

Jeff couldn't imagine what it could be. Then he realized Matt was out-of-uniform.

They'd both been given uniforms by the Diddington Hall hospital's Quartermaster when they were discharged from the hospital - based on their rank when they were admitted - to wear to the Flak House and back to base. Matt, who had been promoted to an officer while in the hospital, was still wearing an enlisted man's uniform.

Jeff started removing Matt's uniforms from his locker, and stuffing them into Matt's empty B-4 flyer's luggage bag, joked,

"You need to trade these in for officer's uniforms before we report to Captain Hancock, or he'll turn you in for impersonating an enlisted man."

But Jeff's joke didn't have the effect that he'd hoped for. Matt was now clearly upset, and Jeff thought he knew why.

Unlike Jeff, who'd been an officer for almost a year and had made the transition from Air Cadet to Second Lieutenant with most of his graduating class, Matt had never experienced being an officer before and was transitioning from enlisted man to officer by himself. He wasn't trained to be an officer, didn't know how to comport himself, and his introverted nature wasn't going to help. But Jeff also thought Matt had an even greater concern. So, he pulled Matt in a close embrace, with their foreheads touching, and began to gently rub his back, before saying, in a soothing voice,

"You promised you'd tell me if something was bothering you.

"You're worried about meeting Wes and the other guys on your line crew, aren't you?"

Matt nodded yes, so Jeff asked,

"Why, Matt? Wes is your biggest fan. I bet he's bursting at the seams, itching for the chance to be the first one to salute you."

Matt tried to calm himself before answering.

"As a sergeant-pilot, I didn't fit in with either the officers or the enlisted guys. That, and being a little awkward, isolated me when the Group first arrived here, to the point where I'd spend days not speaking to anyone.

"Wes noticed me hanging around the flight line one day, watching his crew from a distance change an engine, and asked if I'd like to help. When I said yes, he told me to grab his toolbox and a pair of overalls and join his crew. Then he told the members of his crew to put me to work.

"At first, they'd give me small jobs to do, like changing the spark plugs, but eventually, I learned how to do most of the maintenance on the P-38, including tearing-down and rebuilding an engine. I loved working with the guys and Wes so much.

"I became really good at safety wiring - you know, the tedious method they use of twisting fine steel wire to prevent the fasteners from loosening from vibration, something the guys don't like to do, but that Wes is a stickler about - so I'd volunteer to help whenever a lot of safety wiring needed to be done.

"Wes and I became close friends - really, he was my only friend, more like an older brother. He took me under his wing; I would have been lost here without him.

"There's one more thing. I really respect Wes as a mechanic. I know some pilots joke that the mechanic's motto is, "Beat it to fit and paint it to match," but it's not true. Those guys are incredibly responsible and care about their pilots a lot.

"I'm convinced Wes' unauthorized tweaks to my P-38, and his additional, unscheduled maintenance - like examining the spark plugs and doing compression checks after every mission - is the reason we made it back from the Berlin mission: I was able to exceed all the limits on the engine and airframe and get away with it, because of him.

"I respect his advice so much. He's helped me survive here and even got me to trust you," as Matt displayed his medallion.

"And now, the thought of out-ranking him, having him salute me and call me sir, really bothers me a lot. It's like I don't appreciate everything that he's done for me. I don't know if I can face him."

Matt paused for a moment, trying not to break down, then added what was probably bothering him the most,

WILLARD - MUSTANG WINGMAN -34

"And I'm going to miss having him as my friend. We can't just hang out together anymore, or we'll be turned-in for fraternizing, and I could get him into trouble."

Jeff let Matt get it all out before responding.

"Ok, Matt. I understand now why you're upset. But trust me; you've wound yourself up for nothing. I'll help you through this. I'm a pro at this by now; just follow my lead.

"First, there's no saluting on the flight line. Remember? The only time Wes or the rest of your crew would have to salute you is if they ran into you near Headquarters or the other admin buildings.

"Peer to peer, officers of the same rank never salute each other. We'll return a salute if someone initiates it, but mostly we only salute higher-ranking officers. It's pretty much what you did before, except you'll probably salute less because you don't have to salute anyone with the rank of First Lieutenant or below, and that's most of the guys you'll run into on base.

Thomas Willard © 2021

"And how you address the crew and they address you goes, you can do as I do: I call my guys by their first names unless there is high-ranking brass around, which is practically never.

"They do have to call you sir, but I give my crew one sir a day, total, that's it. Any more, and I have a private talk with my crew chief telling him I'm uncomfortable, and we need to lighten things up. They won't sir you to death, but they can't call you by your first name either, though my crew chief does when no one else is around. So, what they do is not address you at all: they leave your name and sir out when they are speaking to you.

"Trust me, Wes and your guys know how to act around the brass. They'll switch into official-mode quickly on their own.

"And as far as hanging out with Wes goes, you can't get Wes in trouble for fraternizing: you're the one that would be in trouble if anyone reported you two for being too friendly.

"But really, it would come down to Colonel Crowell - if he wanted to charge you - and believe me, that's the last thing he cares about. I think he'd point you and your crew out as the best example of pilot-and-line-crew cooperation if the issue ever came up.

"You're not going to be able to work with your crew anymore on the plane, but you're going to be busy doing other things, like helping to plan missions, leading flights, and training new pilots, so you wouldn't have the time anyway. Wes and your crew will understand.

"You can always pull Wes aside and have a private talk; there's no law against it. And you could invite him to the Officer's Club for a beer, or he can invite you to the NCO Club, where he'd probably feel more comfortable.

"I like and respect my crew chief, Mike, a lot, but now I like Wes, too; I actually think of him as a friend, but I'm not sure if he feels the same way; I hope he does.

"When we meet our crews for the first time, everyone will be allowed a few minutes of informal greeting, with hugs, handshakes, and back-slapping – we're human, we've all been through a lot - before we have to switch back to semi-official mode.

"I promise, by then, there will be nothing but smiles. I'll have hugged my guys, your guys, and especially Wes, and hopefully, you'll have, too. And I'll be right next to you, with my arm around your shoulder."

Matt smiled at the thought and at the smooch Jeff gave him as he finished. Jeff had removed the dread he'd been feeling, putting another of his irrational fears to rest.

When Matt seemed more composed, Jeff said,

"There's something you can do for your guys.

"You've never taken even partial credit for any kills. I've seen you make strikes on planes, even shoot them down, and allow credit to go to another pilot, who probably didn't realize you had helped with the kill.

"Because of that, your plane has no victory marks painted on the nose. Your guys probably haven't told you, but they get ranked on by the other crews for still having a naked plane.

"You've been credited with two kills from the Berlin mission. Ask Wes to paint two victory marks on the nose and finally give your crew some bragging rights. It will make their day."

Matt shook his head yes, then hugged Jeff, wondering what he'd ever done to deserve to be friends with this amazing guy.

They exchanged Matt's enlisted men's uniforms for a set of officers with the Quartermaster, then returned to the barracks so Matt could change. Jeff supervised Matt's dressing, making sure everything was in regulation, and helped Matt tie his tie. A beaming Jeff had the honor of pinning one of the First Lieutenant silver bars Colonel Jenkins had given Matt in the hospital on the right-collar of his shirt, making him officially an officer. Then Jeff, trying to eliminate any fear Matt still had about receiving his first salute, stole the honor of First Salute for himself and saluted Matt, who saluted him back, then hugged him.

Jeff, sensing the relief in Matt, said, "Good, that's out of the way."

Thomas Willard © 2021

They reported to Captain Hancock, who warmly welcomed them back. He told them the Group was really busy, so busy that it had been divided into two sub-groups, A and B, so it could support multiple missions at once. And half the pilots were new, with little time in a P-38 or in combat. He was going to need them to help bring the new pilots up to speed and to lead flights on missions.

Before he could put them on the pilot roster, though, he needed them to check themselves and their new planes out. The planes were Lockheed's latest model, the first in the Group, the P-38J-25-LO - equipped with electrically actuated dive recovery flaps to alleviate the compressibility problem and hydraulically boosted ailerons to greatly increase the roll rate – and had just been delivered from the depot. He needed them to take them up and flight test them to verify they were combat-ready.

He handed them each a P-38J flight manual and told them when they were ready, to go to the Ready Room and suit-up, then ask one of the drivers stationed there to take them to their planes; their planes shared the same loop hardstand in the 38th's dispersal area along the perimeter track. He'd notify their line crews they were coming and call the control tower to authorize their flights.

Matt and Jeff walked the short distance to the Ready Room, where the pilot lockers with all their flight gear were located, found their lockers, and changed into their flight gear. Then they sought out one of the drivers on duty and asked to be taken out to the 38th's dispersal area.

As the jeep that they were riding in approached their planes and they saw their two line crews waiting, Matt's apprehension returned. But when Jeff leaped from the back of the jeep and began hugging his crew, Matt saw the scene Jeff had imagined begin to play out, and sure enough, he was quickly surrounded by his and Jeff's crews, and for a few moments, ranked didn't matter, as they both were mauled by every member of both crews.

After they'd enjoyed a few minutes of private celebration, Jeff, to get things back to semi-official, cleared his throat and said to his crew chief,

"Mike, ah, Sergeant Wentworth. Is she all set for a test flight?"

Mike, smiling, happy to have his pilot back, said, "Yes, sir. She's fully fueled and pre-checked. I ran her up to operating temperature about 15 minutes ago."

Matt looked at Wes and, still with a little trepidation in his voice, asked, " Sergeant Potts, is our ship ready?"

Wes, with a broad smile, proudly said, " Yes, sir. She's been fueled and pre-flighted. And I warmed the engines about 15 minutes ago as well."

Jeff looked at Matt and nodded at Wes in encouragement.

"Hmm, Wes. We've been credited with two kills from the Berlin flight. When you get a chance, could you paint two victory-marks on wherever you think is best," then added, "And if you and the crew decide what you'd like to see for nose art, you're welcome to paint that on as well; whatever you come up with is good."

When his crew went wild with excitement, Matt looked at Jeff, who, smiling with satisfaction, just shook his head up and down in agreement.

#

CELEBRATION

Matt and Jeff each pulled their crew chiefs aside for a private conversation.

Matt thanked Wes for all his past help, telling him how grateful he was. Then he thanked Wes for his medallion - pulling it from his pocket to show it – and for his personal advice about Jeff, that he'd taken it, and that Wes had been right about everything. He told him he wanted to stay friends and that he'd try to work around any barriers. And that if Wes or anyone on the line crew ever needed his support or had any idea that needed visibility, to let him know, and he'd do everything he could to see that it made it up the food-chain.

Thomas Willard © 2021

Wes helped Matt into the cockpit and reviewed the small differences between the P-38H model Matt was used to flying, to the P-38J. They agreed that Matt should avoid using the new dive recovery flap feature for this first test flight – no high-speed, greater than 400 mph dives - but to try and cover the rest of the combat flight envelope to be sure everything operated at least as well as the P-38H.

Matt missed flying and was excited to try the new plane. He'd heard that the new hydraulically-assisted ailerons had greatly increased the roll rate, putting the P-38 in the same league as the Spitfire and ME 109 when it came to tight-turn maneuvering.

He waited while Wes plugged all the electrical jacks in, connected the oxygen hose, and buckled and tightened the safety harness straps. Wes then patted Matt on the shoulder and helped close the cockpit canopy before using the ladder to climb off the back of the wing and storing the ladder in the rear of the center-fuselage gondola.

Matt was about to start his engines when he radioed Jeff to see if he was ready. When there was no response, Matt looked at Jeff's plane and noticed Mike hadn't made as much progress strapping Jeff in. And then he thought he saw a concerned look on Mike's face.

Matt gestured to Wes to go over and ask Mike if everything was alright. When Wes came back, he lowered the ladder and climbed back up the wing to Matt. By then, Matt had lowered the window on the bottom section of the canopy so he could speak with Wes.

Wes told him that something had come over Jeff, that he seemed disoriented and scared, and that Mike was trying to calm him down, but it wasn't working.

Matt raised the canopy and asked Wes to help unbuckle his harness. When he was free, Wes helped Matt out of the cockpit, and Matt climbed down off the wing and walked to Jeff's plane.

Mike, relieved to see Matt approaching, climbed down to meet him. He started,

"Lieutenant Yetman," but Matt stopped him.

"Mike, no one's here. It's Matt, OK. What's wrong?"

"Everything was fine until I started buckling him in and started describing the new features. Then something happened to him. I could tell he wasn't following me, and then I noticed he was shaking. I've never seen Jeff scared before. I don't know what to do."

"For right now, let's act like nothing's wrong; keep this just between us. I'm going up to talk with him." Seeing a worried look on Mike's face, he said,

"Trust me. I won't try to talk him into flying. I won't let him fly if I don't think it's safe; I'll take his keys. We'll invent a mechanical issue if we have to, OK?"

Mike nodded yes, and gave his crew some busy work to keep them distracted while Matt climbed up to speak with Jeff.

Matt looked in the cockpit and found a defeated-looking Jeff staring out the front windscreen. When Jeff saw Matt, he offered a brave smile, but Matt knew it was for his benefit and saw through it.

Matt started, "Hey Jeff, how's it going? Is everything alright?"

Jeff tried to slough off his fear and said, "I'll be fine; just give me a minute."

Matt said, "You promised to tell me if something was bothering you."

Jeff smiled, realizing Matt had stolen his line.

"Something's wrong, Jeff. It's me. No one else can hear. If you need more time, I'll say I don't feel well, and we can go back to the barracks and try again some other time."

When Jeff didn't respond, Matt decided to end the check flight and started to call Mike over to let him know, but Jeff stopped him.

"I was fine until I started to climb into the cockpit. Then I had a flashback of the crash and froze.

"I think if I get out now, I'll never get back in again."

Matt was angry at himself. He'd been so excited about getting to fly again that he hadn't even thought about how Jeff's crash might have resulted in emotional trauma for him, that Jeff, rather than being excited about flying again, might now be terrified of it. So, he shared that thought with Jeff.

"I'm sorry. I should have realized this wouldn't be the same for you. I'm like a selfish little kid getting to play with a new toy while you're reliving a nightmare.

"We can get out of this easy. We'll blame it all on me; I'm the one that's scared. Then you can say I scared you, and they'll ground the both of us."

Jeff smiled at Matt's crazy scheme. He knew Matt would do it if he didn't stop him, so he asked,

"You're really looking forward to flying this, aren't you? But you'd give up flying for me?"

Matt just said, "Flying is no big deal. It's cold up there, anyway. Maybe they'll give us a warm desk job back in the states."

Jeff's shaking had stopped. He knew how much flying meant to Matt; there was no way he was going to let him get grounded.

"Nope. You're lying, and your plan sucks.

"You just have to help me a little. So, what's different about this plane?"

Matt reviewed the few differences in the P-38 models but was withholding his judgment on whether he'd let Jeff fly.

Jeff asked, "So, why do you think flying this one will be so much better?"

Matt excitedly described what he'd heard about the increase in roll-rate performance. Jeff noticed how enthused Matt was and decided to himself that Matt at least should get a chance to give the plane a try.

When he mentioned that Matt should go up without him, Matt refused, saying,

"Half the fun of going up was to get a chance to fly with you, just us playing around, with no one shooting at us. We've never gotten to do that. I think I was looking forward to that the most."

That made Jeff determined to try again.

"Ok, I want to do that, too. I think I'm better now, and flying with you will get rid of any remaining demons.

"We'll takeoff together, with you flying lead. When we're up there, I'll copy everything you do.

Matt wasn't convinced, worried he'd talked Jeff into flying.

"It's 1430 already, just a couple of hours of daylight left. Why don't we wait until tomorrow?"

But Jeff knew what was bothering Matt and said,

"I'll be fine with you with me. I had forgotten you'd be up there with me before, but now I'm looking forward to flying with you, too. You can't chicken-out on me now."

Matt had noticed Jeff had calmed down and that he wasn't just putting on a brave front for him and said,

"Ok. But we will come right back if you have any problems. I'm trusting you to tell me - we'll use the code word "Spiegel" - and we'll come right back. OK?"

Then he pulled his medallion from his pocket and gave it to Jeff, saying,

"This'll bring you luck. It did for me, or I'd never have gotten to know you."

Then he pulled his oxygen mask from his helmet and said,

"Let's trade masks. I want something of yours, something personal."

They exchanged masks, and after giving Jeff a thumbs up, Matt climbed down from Jeff's plane and returned to his own.

Wes strapped Matt in again, and Mike did the same for Jeff. This time when Matt radioed Jeff to see if he was ready, Jeff replied that he was, and both began starting their engines.

When their engines were warmed up, their crew chiefs pulled the chocks, and Matt asked the tower for taxiing clearance.

As they approached the runway, Matt asked the tower for clearance to takeoff, and when they received it, they taxied to the head of the runway. They both ran a final engine and brake check; then Matt led the way as they took off together, Jeff about 30 feet behind and to the right of him.

Jeff's fears had begun to melt away as soon as he'd put Matt's mask on. Starting the engines dissipated more of his fear, as did taxiing, and as his muscle memory returned. By the time they took off, Jeff was back to enjoying flying again and especially liked being so close to Matt when he was in his element.

Matt, always methodical when flying, did a gradual climb to 15,000 feet to give them plenty of room should they need to pull out of a dive or bailout. Then he cautiously tried some low-G turning maneuvers at a cruise speed of 275 mph. After a half hour without incident, he tried a series of higher-G maneuvers, like barrel rolls for an attack and split-S turns for evasion, with Jeff playing follow the leader.

Satisfied by the plane's performance at medium altitude, Matt climbed to 25,800 feet to see how the plane performed at a higher altitude. There, he adjusted the engine controls to the maximum continuous power settings of 60 inches of mercury and 3000 rpm, reaching a speed of 420 mph before throttling back to 300 mph.

Confident the planes were in good shape, Matt suddenly challenged Jeff, saying,

"Hellcat Red One, I'll race you back to base. The first one with their wheels chocked wins a special prize," and dove for the deck. Jeff, now fully recovered, dove to keep up with Matt.

Matt leveled out at 10,000 feet, and then whenever Jeff was close on his tail, he turned inside to lose him.

Matt was having a ball. The new plane easily turned in half the radius of the older design, with little effort on the controls and without a hint of high-speed stalling.

Jeff was also having fun chasing Matt. He could have just zoomed past Matt whenever he turned and got back to base first, but he decided he'd stay with Matt and let him win; he'd land just behind him.

The race petered out as they turned on final, and they landed together, separated by the same distance as when they'd taken off.

Their line crews were waiting for them when they taxied into their designated hardstand spots. When their engines were stopped and their wheels chocked, their crew chiefs climbed the wings and helped them out of their cockpits.

Once on the ground, Jeff turned to Mike and started to apologize, but Mike was too quick and interrupted him, saying,

"Yes, sir, she handles like a dream. Looks like you two were having fun up there."

By then, Wes and Matt had joined them, but not before Wes had shared some personal information with Matt that he'd just learned from Mike.

Matt put his arm around Jeff's shoulder, then nodded knowingly at Mike before announcing,

WILLARD - MUSTANG WINGMAN -54

"Mike and Wes have invited everyone, including you line crew guys, to the NCO club for a beer to celebrate. It seems that its someone's birthday," pointing at Jeff, "and that's as good an excuse as any."

Later that evening, after celebrating with their crews and dinner, when they'd turned in for bed, Jeff said,

"Thanks for today, Matt. I was pretty far gone this afternoon; I was done flying. I think your offer to play with me up there saved me."

"You were no further gone than I was, worrying about being an officer. Somehow, we know how to help each other."

Jeff, remembering that Matt had won the race, said,

"You won, but I still got the special prize. It doesn't seem fair."

Matt turned sideways to face Jeff and, smiling, said,

"Oh, your birthday celebration was second prize. I still get first prize, and you're it, so lock the door, birthday boy, and get your butt over here."

Thomas Willard © 2021

Jeff just laughed. He thought it was funny Matt was trying to act all-assertive for him, signaling he was feeling frisky. Until then, Matt had never initiated their getting together in bed; it was always Jeff.

Jeff jumped into bed with Matt and then kissed him before lying back to receive his birthday present. What Matt didn't know, and would have panicked if he had, was that in a few minutes, Jeff was going to turn the tables on him and give him an early birthday present of his own, out of love and affection and to keep things even.

CHAPTER 3— START OF SECOND TOUR: MID-JULY 1944

APPEAL

By late February 1944, it was clear that the Allies were winning the pilot-attrition battle. Doolittle and Spaatz's strategy of pressing even the smallest advantage against the Luftwaffe was paying off.

During Big Week, or Operation Argument, from 20 to 24 February 1944, the Allies bombed fighter aircraft manufacturing plants in Germany, forcing the Luftwaffe fighters to respond. The losses on both sides were heavy: 131 RAF bombers, 226 USAAF bombers, and 25 USAAF fighters, versus 262 German fighters. But while the Allied losses were sustainable, the German losses were not. Though Doolittle didn't know it at the time, Big Week broke the back of the Luftwaffe, and they never recovered.

As his bomber and fighter strength continued to grow, Doolittle kept pressing his advantage, and by 4 April 1944, the Allies had gained air superiority over the Channel and most of the Western front, two months before the Normandy invasion.

With the arrival of the new long-range Mustangs in May, and with fighter pilot squadrons at full strength, Doolittle knew if he could convert his fighter squadrons to the technically-superior Mustangs and maintain his advantage in pilots, he'd win the air war. But he was about to experience his own pilot attrition problem.

Pilot tours of duty for the first contingent of pilots from the long-range fighter escort squadrons were about up. If nothing was done, one-third to one-half of his fighter pilots, his most experienced, would soon return to the states.

Doolittle's dilemma was shared by all USAAF commanders in the different Theaters of Operation. As they were just about to gain the upper hand in fighter pilot strength, a large percentage of their pilots were due to return home.

Though no universal standard for pilot rotation existed among the commands, the general rule was a pilot was eligible for rotation after 200 hours of combat flight time. And though never expressly stated, pilots interpreted the rules to mean rotation was certain after 200 combat hours, and they couldn't be required to serve a second combat tour, though state-side duty was expected.

This USAAF tour-of-duty rule contrasted sharply with the Luftwaffe's, which had no limit on pilot combat hours: a pilot flew until he was killed, captured, or severely injured.

In January 1944, when fighter squadrons were still not at full strength, and the Air Force was having trouble just keeping up with pilot attrition, the Commander of the USAAF, General "Hap" Arnold, ordered his commanders to rescind all tour-of-duty rules, stated or implied. The new standard was pilots would continue to fly until they were judged to be so fatigued they impacted the effectiveness of their unit.

When Doolittle issued his version of this order to the Eighth Air Force, their reaction was as he expected. The pilots felt the goal-posts had moved, that their chances of surviving the war had greatly been reduced. Without a goal to shoot for, pilot morale plummeted, so the commanders pushed back.

Bowing to this pressure, Arnold revised his order, leaving it to his commanders to establish their own tour-of-duty criteria.

Doolittle tweaked the Eighth's tour-of-duty rules several times over the next six months.

He didn't want to lose the numerical superiority of skilled pilots the pilot's themselves had sacrificed so much to achieve, but he knew maintaining their morale was just as important.

So, he attacked the tour-of-duty problem in three stages, from less to more coercive.

First, in June 1944, he issued a letter making a personal appeal to pilots eligible to rotate at the end of the month to voluntarily sign-up for a second tour-of-duty. That resulted in about half the eligible pilots extending their tours, but he held up the rotation of the remaining pilots.

In July, he issued another letter, again appealing to any pilots eligible to rotate in June or July to voluntarily sign-up for a second tour, but this time adding that only lower combat-hour pilots and those that signed-up would be eligible to train on the new Mustangs. That resulted in half the hold-outs from June and three-quarters of July's pilots signing up, but he still held up the rotation of the June and July hold-outs.

Then in August 1944, he issued another order, this time rescinding all prior tour-of-duty rules. The new rule was there was no longer a combat-hour maximum. Instead, pilots would continue to fly until they were judged to be so greatly fatigued as to endanger the effectiveness of their unit. However, no pilot with over 300 hours would be required to fly combat without first being evaluated for fitness.

By the time he'd issued his order in August, most of the fighter pilots eligible to rotate had voluntarily signed-up for a second tour. He'd kept the hard-won pilot numerical advantage, which, in the long run, he thought would save pilot lives, without sacrificing the morale of his pilots. He vowed to himself, though, to send second-tour fighter pilots home as soon as possible.

#

SUBTERFUGE

When Matt first learned of Doolittle's appeal in June, he decided to sign-up for a second tour, but to keep his decision a secret from Jeff: he didn't want Jeff to sign-up; he wanted him to go back to the states.

Matt was waiting for a chance to break-away from Jeff for an hour or two, so he could visit Group Headquarters and complete the paperwork without Jeff noticing. But, between daily missions, and their nearly exact schedules, no opportunity presented itself until his birthday on the 2nd of July, when Jeff seemed like he was trying to ditch him.

It was one of the rare days they had free, and Jeff had gotten up early before Matt and left a note saying he'd be back in a few hours.

Matt got up, dressed, and ate breakfast before visiting Colonel Crowell's office. There, he filled out the paperwork volunteering for a second tour but asked the Group's adjutant not to post his name on the list of volunteers who'd signed up for a second tour.

When he got back to the barracks, he found a second note from Jeff, saying he was sorry he'd missed him but that he'd be back in an hour or so.

Matt was napping when Jeff returned. Jeff went to Matt's bed, bent down, then kissed him, saying,

"Happy Birthday, sleepy head. You need to get up. We have a 24-hour pass, and I have plans for you."

Matt, who didn't think Jeff knew when his birthday was, was all smiles and kissed Jeff back, asking,

"So, what are we up to?"

"We're staying tonight at the White Hart Inn, about five miles away in Halstead. They're not sure how old the place is, but they guess it was built in the 13th century. Being from Boston, I know you like all the old history stuff.

"They have great food and real ale: you're 21 now, so no more 3.2 beer for you. I plan to get you drunk for the first time. My guess is it will take two pints at the most."

Matt was hugging Jeff when there was a knock at the door. They separated, and Jeff said, "Come in."

Captain Hancock entered. When Matt and Jeff started to salute, he waved them off.

"I just want to thank you two for signing-up for a second tour. I know a lot of guys are going to follow your lead.

"Jeff finagled your 24-hour leave this morning, Matt. I've never been to the White Hart Inn. I don't know how he managed to get you booked in there. I'm jealous.

"When you get back tomorrow, I'd like you both to report to my office. I want to get you guys checked-out on the P-51 tomorrow afternoon. The whole Group is going to convert to Mustangs by the middle of the month."

Then Captain Hancock thanked them again before leaving.

Matt, who'd managed to hide his emotions until the Captain had left, was so furious with Jeff for signing up that he couldn't even look at him.

Jeff, knowing this was how Matt would react, speaking to Matt's back, tried to explain.

"Matt, I know you're mad at me. I was going to tell you. But I didn't want you to find out today, on your birthday.

"When I came back earlier and missed you, I knew what you'd done, so I went over to Group Headquarters and signed-up, too.

"You can be mad at me for not telling you first, but you signed-up without telling me. If you had, I would have tried to talk you out of it, but then I'd have snuck over to Group and signed-up without you, hoping you wouldn't find out until you were about to be rotated. You would have probably done the same thing. So why are you so mad at me?"

Matt, trying to calm himself down, said,

"I was so happy you were going home, that one of us was going to make it.

" Almost half the guys that came over with us last October are gone, dead or a POW.

"The odds that one of us, let alone both of us, are going to survive are ridiculously small.

"I wanted at least one of us to make it: I wanted it to be you."

Jeff, relieved that Matt was at least talking to him, said,

"I'm not going to leave here without you.

"I'm just like you; I want to help end the war and get Colonel Jenkins and all the other POW pilots we know released as soon as possible. And I want a chance to fly the Mustang.

"I know the odds suck, but we have an advantage: we have each other.

"And I don't just mean in combat. I mean in the times between, when we can relax together, actually enjoy life a little, with each other. No one else has that. We're very lucky."

Matt, a little more composed, said,

"Do you think they'd let us withdraw our sign-ups?"

Jeff said, "No, not now after they've made plans to use us as poster-boys for volunteering. Besides, do you really want to?"

Matt thought about it and decided it was too late to withdraw. But he wanted some assurance from Jeff that he'd be more careful in combat.

"You have to be more careful, take fewer risks. We promised Colonel Crowell we'd set a good example."

Jeff said, "I can't promise that. It's better to be too aggressive than indecisive. We only have a split-second to make decisions in combat. It's more operating on instinct than with a plan."

But then Jeff made a compromise.

"You don't like hearing this, but you have great instincts based on your amazing situational awareness. No one reads a situation better than you. And you've studied the strengths and weaknesses of the different fighters, so you know when you have the advantage and should engage and when you should break-off.

"You can help me do better at assessing the situation. I'm not talking about second-guessing myself. I mean sharpening my instincts so they are based on the best odds of winning in a dogfight.

"How about that; are you game?"

Matt didn't accept that he was a better pilot than Jeff in any way. But he thought they'd both benefit from some mock-combat practice sessions.

"I'm no genius when it comes to figuring out the best odds. But maybe we could talk about things a little, especially since we'll be converting soon to Mustangs."

Jeff, sensing the storm had passed, said,

"Looks like we're going to be stuck here together for a while longer," and gave his best puppy-dog-eyes expression, then kissed Matt on the cheek. He locked the door and started to unbutton his shirt, planning on seducing Matt.

Matt said, "Oh, brother," and while rolling his eyes, kicked off his shoes, trying but failing to resist Jeff's charm offensive.

#

SWITCH TO MUSTANGS

Matt and Jeff had a great time at the White Hall Inn. Knowing they would be flying the next day, Jeff minimized their drinking, limiting them both to one pint of ale, which was more than enough to get Matt loopy.

They returned to base by noon the next day, then reported to Captain Hancock. They were each given a copy of the P-51D's flight manual, then instructed to go to the Ready Room to put on their flight gear and then ask a driver stationed there to drive them to the 38th Squadron's Mustang training hard-standing area. There, the P-38 pilots finishing their morning training session on the P-51 would check them out on the Mustang.

When they'd arrived at the hard-standing area, the two training Mustangs were just finishing being refueled. The two pilots that had just been checked out that morning on the P-51 individually instructed Matt and Jeff on the Mustang.

After about an hour of ground instruction, the newly-minted instructor-pilots felt Matt and Jeff were ready for a test flight. Since the single-seater fighter had no room for an instructor, they would fly solo on their first flight.

The line crews helped strap Matt and Jeff into their planes, and then they both started the engines. After engine warm-up, they asked the control tower for taxiing clearance, and with Jeff leading, they taxied to the head of the runway.

Once there, they requested takeoff clearance, and when granted, they taxied to the head of the runway. There, they did a final engine and brake check, then they set the engine controls to takeoff power and headed down the runway.

Unlike the P-38 with counter-rotating engines that eliminated engine torque, the powerful single P-51 Merlin engine produced significant torque, trying to roll the plane to the left, requiring right, opposite aileron input with the control stick to counter.

With that one exception, Matt and Jeff found the P-51 was a dream to fly, and after some initially cautious turns and dives, they spent the remainder of the two-hour check-out flight just having fun.

They had to remember how to land a tail-dragger, but since that was what they had initially learned on, it was second nature to them.

When they'd landed and were pulling into the loop hard-standing area, they found another pair of P-38 pilots waiting to be checked-out. Now it was their turn to act as instructor-pilots, and for the next hour, they each trained a pilot. They stayed and watched as their new Mustang student-pilots took off before getting a ride back to the Ready Room to change.

#

55TH MUSTANGS FIRST COMBAT: ESCORT TO MUNICH: 21 JULY 1944

On 7th July 1944, the 55th Fighter Group flew its last mission using P-38s. The mission, to escort 90 Second Bomb Division B-24s to Bernburg, Germany, bombing the Junkers engine and aircraft works, was led by Major Wendell Kelly and consisted of 46 P-38s from the 38th, 338th, and 343rd Fighter Squadrons. Rendezvous with the bombers was at 0835 at 24,000 feet near Bersenbruck, Germany.

The Germans were out in force defending the target. At 1000, about 20 minutes to the target, near Hildesheim, Germany, the 38th Squadron encountered a force of 30 ME 410s at 16,000 feet heading towards the bombers.

The ensuing air battle was ferocious but resulted in the loss of 18 enemy fighters, with no 55th Fighter Group fighters lost.

From the 8th to the 20th of July, the 55th converted to P-51D Mustangs. The Group's pilots either took leave, helped ferry planes to and from the depot airfields, or trained on the P-51s.

For its first mission with Mustangs, on 21 July 1944, escorting B-24 bombers from the 2nd and 3rd Bomb Divisions to the Dornier aircraft factory in Munich, Germany, the 55th Fighter Group split into two combat units: A Group, led by Colonel Crowell, with 18 P-51s from the 338th Squadron, and 9 P-51s from the 343rd Squadron; and B Group, led by Major John Landers, with 17 P-51s from the 38th Squadron, and nine from the 343rd Squadron.

Both groups of fighters rendezvoused with the bombers near Karlsruhe, Germany, at 0945 and 25,000 feet. The target was concealed by clouds, and after escorting the bombers over the target, the formation was attacked by a group of ME 109s.

The new Mustangs proved more than a match for the 109s, which were heavier now after a redesign and less maneuverable, and, because of severe fuel shortages due to the success of Allied strategic bombing, reduced to using lower-octane synthetic fuel.

Both Matt and Jeff scored a kill, bringing each of their totals to

four.

CHAPTER 4 — RAMROD TO RUHLAND: 11 SEPTEMBER 1944

MISSION 623: OVERVIEW

Though always considered an important strategic target, from 3 to 13 September 1944, the Eighth Air Force concentrated its bombing missions on German oil refineries and synthetic oil plants.

On 11 September 1944, the Eighth Air Force launched Mission 623, dispatching a force of 1,131 bombers and 440 fighters, on three routes to ten separate primary targets, deep into Germany to hit oil refineries and synthetic oil plants. That force encountered an estimated 525 Luftwaffe fighters, with a US loss of

40 bombers and 17 fighters, against the German loss of 132 fighters.

This was the largest air battle for the 55th Fighter Group during WWII and became known as "The Air Battle Over Ore Mountain."

The 55th Fighter Group was assigned escort duty for the B-17 bombers from the 100th Bombardment Group and provided a total of 48 P-51 Mustangs - from the 38th, 338th, and 343rd Fighter Squadrons.

The 100th Bombardment Group - part of the 3rd Air Division and comprised of a total of 54 B-17s from the 349th, 350th, 351st, and 418th Bombardment Squadrons – was tasked with bombing the Schwarzheide synthetic oil factory in Ruhland, Germany, near the German-Czechoslovakian border.

The mission proceeded without incident until the formation reached Oberhof, Germany, in the Thuringian Forest mountain range, about 45 miles southwest of Erfurt. There, a group of approximately 50 ME 109 Luftwaffe fighters from II Gruppe,

Jagdgeschwader 4, jumped the two fighter squadrons patrolling about 20 miles ahead of the bombers to clear the skies of enemy fighters– the 38th and the 338th - beginning the first phase of the battle.

The P-51s managed to fight off the ME 109s – with no loss of bombers, but a loss of two P-51s, versus a loss of 6 ME 109s - but had to jettison their drop tanks early, so they needed to return to base. That left only the 16 fighters of the 343rd Squadron with enough fuel to escort the bombers to and from the target.

About 30 minutes later, near present-day Kovarska, Czechoslovakia, the second phase of the battle occurred. The formation was attacked again by fighters of II Gruppe but was now joined by approximately 50 FW 190 fighters from III Gruppe, for a total of 100 German fighters against 16 US fighters.

The result was the loss of 14 B-17s and two additional P-51s. But, because of the bravery and fierceness of the 343rd pilots and the B-17 gun crews, the Germans lost an additional 31 fighters, for a total of 37 German fighters - and maybe more importantly, 29 pilots - lost.

In recognition of its outstanding valor in a series of aerial battles between 3 and 13 September 1944, the 55th Fighter Group was awarded its first Distinguished Unit Citation (DUC).

#

PRE-BRIEFING PREPARATION

Alerted the night before they would be part of the next day's mission, Matt and Jeff were awoken at 0645 by a knock on the door by the Group's Intelligence Officer, telling them to report to the Briefing Room at 0830.

They had both slept in just their boxers and a t-shirt but now added a pair of woolen long johns and two pairs of socks. Then, they put on their "pink," drab olive shade 54 woolen pants, chocolate woolen shirt, brown canvas belt, khaki tie, and brown shoes before visiting the latrine.

Once they finished washing and brushing their teeth, they returned to the barracks and climbed into their olive-drab cotton twill L-1 overall flight suit. The left thigh of the flight suit had a 4-inch by 4-inch clear glassine patch covering a mini-map of Germany; the right shin had a zippered-cargo pocket that held the escape kit; and the left shin pocket held a sheathed knife.

They strapped on their shoulder holster with a loaded .45-caliber revolver, put on an A-2 flight jacket and an officer's cap, and then headed for the officer's mess hall.

At a time of severe food rationing in the US and England, USAAF and RAF pilots were fed well. Matt and Jeff each ate a hearty breakfast of orange juice, oatmeal with heavy cream, scrambled eggs, pan-fried potatoes, SOS, and hot cocoa. They ate all of that for two reasons; first, so that they wouldn't get hungry during the up to six-hour flight, and second, to survive longer without eating just in case they were shot down and needed to escape.

After breakfast, they walked to the Briefing Room, a few huts away.

#

MISSION BRIEFING

When they arrived, they found the room full with 48 pilots from all three of the 55th Fighter Group's squadrons - the 38th Squadron, radio call sign Hellcat; the 338th Squadron, call sign Acorn; and the 343rd Squadron, call sign Tudor - seated on a dozen long wooden benches. At promptly 0830, the room was called to attention, and Lieutenant Colonel John McGinn, who would lead the mission, began the briefing.

The day's mission was another deep penetration into Germany, this time escorting 54 B-17s from the 100th Bombardment Group. Their target was the synthetic fuel plant in Ruhland, Germany, near the Czechoslovakian border. Even with drop tanks, fuel-management was going to be crucial.

The straight-line distance to the target was 560 miles, but adding the dog-leg feints to obscure the bomber's target and fuel for dogfighting, this was going to be at or near the endurance limit of the P-51 Mustangs.

The Mustangs had three internal fuel tanks: an 85-gallon auxiliary tank in the fuselage behind the cockpit, which, to keep the center of gravity within limits, was restricted to 40 gallons for combat maneuvering; and two 92-gallon fuel tanks, one in each wing. In addition, two 108-gallon paper external drop tanks, one below each wing, could be added to extend the range. The total was 485 gallons, giving the P-51 a maximum range of 1650 miles at a cruising speed of 275 mph and a maximum endurance of six hours.

Taxiing would be at 0930; rendezvous with the bombers at 1040 at 24,000 feet near Verviers, Belgium; escort of the bombers to the target at 1220 and on return until drop-off near Verviers at 1400; then landing at 1450.

The weather would be clear for takeoff and landing, with some light cloud cover over the target expected.

During the briefing, the pilots used a crayon to plot the route, heading, and timing information onto their glassine-covered mini-maps.

Before finishing the briefing, the Colonel synchronized their watches. Then, all the pilots walked the short distance to the Ready Room hut to learn their flight assignments and to suit-up.

#

READY ROOM

The Ready Room was where the pilots learned their mission flight assignments from the Scheduling board and where they suited-up. It held the pilot's personal lockers, storing their flight gear, and it was also where the pilots turned in their personal items – mostly their wallets, but anything that could provide personal information to the enemy if they were captured - to one of the Group's Intelligence officers.

Matt and Jeff looked at the 38th Squadron's Scheduling Board and saw that they each would be leading a flight: Matt would lead Red Flight, and Jeff would lead White Flight.

After turning in their personal items, they went to their lockers to don their flight gear. They each exchanged their brown A-2 leather jacket for the much warmer olive-drab B-15 and their shoes for a pair of black, fleece-lined RAF 1943-pattern escape boots.

They put their escape kit – containing K-rations, aspirin, water purifier, matches, and a dime-sized compass - into the left cargo pocket of their flight suit, then put their yellow B-3 life preserver on over their jacket.

Next, they put their black leather A-11 helmet - equipped with earphones - on, and then their black rubber B-8 goggles over their helmet.

They attached their black rubber A-14 oxygen face mask - equipped with an internal microphone - to the strap at the bottom left of the helmet and then connected its rubber hose to the face mask, leaving the other end, which connected to the plane's oxygen supply, dangling near their waist.

They put on a pair of black leather A-11 gloves, then strapped-on their backpack-like B-8 parachute - with an RAF first-aid kit hanging by a lanyard from the bottom - leaving the leg straps loose so they could still walk.

Finally, they hung a "Blood Chit" placard, written in several languages, that sported an American flag, declaring that the bearer was a service member of the USAAF and requesting that he be provided any assistance necessary, promising a reward for delivering the service man to safety.

When they'd finished suiting-up, they were both about 40 pounds heavier. Barely able to walk, they waddled to a truck waiting to take them and several other pilots to their planes.

At 0930 - after preflight inspection and engine warmup – the Group took off, forming and climbing to 15,000 feet over the Channel at the P-51's cruise speed of 275 mph, on a heading of

135 degrees, on route to their first waypoint: the lighthouse on the shore at Nieuwpoort, Belgium.

#

BATTLE OF ORE MOUNTAIN: FIRST PHASE

As the Group neared Verviers, Belgium, and they started their climb to 24,000 feet to rendezvous with the bombers at 1040, Colonel McGinn, call sign Windsor and leading Acorn Yellow Flight, selected Acorn and Hellcat Squadrons to provide loose-escort for the bombers – flying a screen 10 to 20 miles ahead, to clear the skies of any enemy fighters before they could reach the bombers - leaving Tudor Squadron to provide close-escort fighter protection for the bombers.

The formation proceeded normally until 1145, when Colonel McGinn sighted contrails at 30,000 feet over the town of Oberhof, in the Thuringian Forest mountain range, near Erfurt, Germany.

The Colonel ordered Acorn and Hellcat Squadrons to jettison their drop tanks. Then, as he ordered both squadrons, totaling 32 Mustangs, to turn starboard to attack out of the sun, two ME 109s out of the main force of 50 attacked Acorn Squadron from the eight-o'clock position, scattering the two squadrons of Mustangs.

The ensuing dogfight was the first phase of the fiercest battle the 55th Fighter Group fought during WWII. Outnumbered almost two-to-one, fighting on the enemy's turf, the Acorn and Hellcat Squadrons managed to fight off the attack, scoring six kills with no bombers lost but losing two P-51s from Hellcat Squadron in return.

When the dogfight, which lasted less than five minutes, was over, Colonel McGinn radioed for all Acorn and Hellcat fighters to reassemble at 8000 feet. Because they'd had to jettison their drop tanks early – leaving them without enough fuel to make it to the target and back to base – and because they had already exhausted nearly all their ammunition fighting off the ME 109s, the Colonel, unable to foresee that the worst of the fighting was yet to come in the second stage of the battle at Kovarska - with nearly 100 enemy fighters against just 16 Mustangs of the 343rd - ordered the two squadrons to return to base.

Matt and Jeff - who had survived the battle, along with all the members of their flights - had each scored a kill in the dogfight, giving them each a total of 5 kills and making them both Aces.

#

ZOOM-CLIMB RAM

The return flight was uneventful until Matt, flying two miles ahead of Jeff's flight and in sight of the Channel, spotted a severely damaged, unescorted B-17 straggler about 3000 feet above them at 18,000 feet, with both starboard-side engines out, and with smoke coming from the port-side inboard engine, struggling to maintain a 135-mph air speed. As Matt approached the bomber from behind, its six o'clock position, and got within a half mile of the bomber, he noticed a bandit, an ME 109, two miles ahead at the same

Thomas Willard © 2021

altitude as the bomber and at the bomber's twelve o'clock position, heading straight at it and closing fast.

The P-51D had six Browning AN/M2 machine guns mounted in the wings, each firing at a rate of 800 rounds per minute, with a standard convergence setting of 300 yards. The two inboard guns had 400 rounds each, while the four outer guns had 270 rounds each, for a total of 1880 rounds. All the guns fired simultaneously by pulling the trigger on the control stick, with a total of 30 seconds of firing: 20 seconds of six-gun firing, with an additional ten seconds of two-gun firing. There was no indicator to show the number of rounds remaining: the pilot kept track by counting how many seconds he'd fired.

Matt checked with his flight to see if anyone had any ammunition left, but everyone except the rookie in the tail-end Charlie position thought they had used most of their ammo up.

He thought that he had at most two seconds of firing remaining, or about 52 rounds left, but decided to go for the bandit anyway, thinking that he might be able to scare the bandit off or lure him into a dogfight away from the bomber. So, he warned his relatively inexperienced flight wingman,

"Hellcat Red One to Red Two. I'm going after the bandit, but it's going to be close; I'll have to be quick. Get them home as soon as possible. Don't wait around for me to rejoin you. Over."

Matt's flight wingman replied,

"Roger Red One. Don't worry about us; we'll be fine from here. Good luck."

By then, Matt had pushed the throttle to War Emergency Power, breaking the safety wire restricting its use, which set the manifold pressure to 67 inches of mercury and the engine speed to 3000 rpm for an engine power setting of 1695 hp. Then he increased the manifold pressure even further, beyond the rating of the engine, to 75 inches of mercury and the engine speed to 3650 rpm for an engine power setting of 2000 hp.

The Mustang quickly accelerated from its cruise speed of 275 mph to the structural-limit speed for that altitude of 410 mph five seconds later, just as Matt passed beneath the bomber 3000 feet above him. Matt continued beyond the bomber another three seconds, 1900 feet ahead, then pulled back hard on the control stick - pulling 4Gs and nearly blacking out – to begin a near-vertical zoom-climb at a rate of 36,000 feet per minute, ten times the plane's maximum rated climb rate, pegging the rate-of-climb indicator and resulting in a five-second climb to 18,000 feet.

The B-17 pilot, a 22-year-old First Lieutenant, had seen the ME 109 lining up for a head-on attack from two miles away. Because of flak and machine gun damage to the bomber's airframe, and the loss of both starboard engines, he couldn't perform any evasive maneuvers: as it was, he was barely able to keep the B-17 in the air. Any dramatic maneuver risked inducing a stall he likely wouldn't recover from.

His gun crew had already exhausted all their ammunition battling fighters over Germany. His co-pilot, radioman, navigator, and bombardier were all injured, so bailing out wasn't an option, at least not for him. And he knew German pilots were trained to aim for the B-17's cockpit.

Desperately, he scanned the airspace in front and to the sides, but he didn't see any "little friends" - Allied fighters - nearby that could save them. So, he took a final look at the picture of his wife taped to the instrument panel and waited for the inevitable. He could see that the ME 109 was nearly in position, only about 400 yards ahead, when he noticed a P-51 rocketing from below, zoom-climbing vertically, 400 yards in front of and below him, firing at the German.

Matt was on a collision course with the bandit: they would collide about 300 yards ahead of the B-17 if he didn't change course soon. He waited until the last possible moment, three seconds before reaching the collision point, before firing his machine guns. When he saw that the German plane remained intact and was in position, ready to fire, Matt - out of ammo and time, knowing he was all that stood between the ten-man bomber crew and their certain death - rather than turning to avoid colliding with the German, deliberately turned into him instead.

The right wing of the Mustang, just outboard of the propeller, impacted the rear fuselage of the ME 109, cutting the tail section completely off. The combined momentum of the Mustang, then climbing at 340 mph, and the ME 109, still flying horizontally at 265 mph, carried the remains of the two planes upwards enough to just clear the B-17 by less than 100 feet.

The German pilot focused on attacking the bomber, but also, due to the blind spot created by his plane's wings, hadn't seen Matt approaching from below. He was closing on the bomber at 400 mph, holding his fire until he was within 300 yards, two seconds away. He was about to pull the trigger when he heard bullets hitting the armor plating beneath him, followed almost immediately by the impact with the Mustang. Looking rearwards, he saw the tail section of the ME 109 was gone, so he quickly jettisoned the canopy and safely bailed out.

The heavily-reinforced leading edge of the Mustang's wing had collided with the lightly-structured tail section of the ME 109, so not as much of the P-51's vertical momentum had been transferred to the German fighter, and the force of the impact had been less than if it had occurred in a more-substantial part of the plane. The result was the Mustang remained mostly intact, though the ME 109's tail wheel had struck the windscreen and canopy of the Mustang, shattering the one-inch-thick laminated safety glass windscreen – which broke but still held together - and damaging the canopy's slide rails and ejector mechanism.

The P-51 continued climbing for another 1500 feet, experienced an aggravated stall at the end of the climb – the right wing stalled first, causing the nose to yaw and fall to the right – then entered a right-hand spin. Matt tried to jettison the canopy, preparing to bail out, but couldn't – the canopy's emergency release mechanism was jammed, and so was the hand crank used to slide the canopy back.

Unable to bail out, his only remaining option was to try to regain control of the plane, following the standard spin-recovery checklist known as PARE for Power to idle; Ailerons to neutral;

Rudder applied opposite the spin and held; and Elevator applied through neutral.

He throttled the engine back to idle to reduce the pitching moment created by the propeller's thrust acting on the horizontal stabilizer, tending to raise the nose and increasing the angle of attack, reinforcing the stall. Then he centered the control stick, returning the ailerons to neutral, helping both wings to reach the same angle of attack and reducing the yaw and pitching moments of the spin. He then applied full left, opposite rudder, further reducing the yaw and pitching moments of the spin. Next, he quickly moved the stick forward, pitching the nose down and reducing the wings' angle of attack to below the critical angle, un-stalling the wings. He was at 8000 feet, quickly approaching the ground, when the plane recovered from the spin. As it did, Matt, now in a steep dive going 300 mph, brought the rudder back to neutral, pulled the stick back to raise the nose, and slowly added power, returning to level flight at 250 mph and 6000 feet.

Matt, badly shaken from the collision, tried to recover and orient himself. The windscreen was so badly cracked he couldn't see through it, but he could see the Channel ahead through the sides of the bubble canopy. The gyro compass was out, so he steered west, towards the Channel, using the backup magnetic compass, on a heading of 270 degrees, in the general direction of Wormingford.

#

WINGMAN AGAIN

Jeff, about two miles behind Matt's flight - which had just reached the bomber - had listened to the radio exchange between Matt and his flight wingman and watched the collision happen in disbelief.

Jeff radioed his flight wingman and said he was going to see if he could find and help Matt and that they should escort the bomber until it was safely across the Channel. Then he raced to catch up with Matt, who he spotted flying at about 6000 feet and heading towards Wormingford.

Still dazed, Matt knew his options were limited. He couldn't see forward, so finding the airfield and landing would be difficult, and his canopy wouldn't open, so he couldn't bail out or ditch - he'd drown trapped in the cockpit. But he knew his radio was still working when he suddenly heard Jeff trying to raise him.

"Hellcat Red One, this is Hellcat White One. Do you read me? Over."

Matt responded,

"Roger White One. Where are you? Over."

"Look out over your left wing, Red One."

When Matt did, he saw Jeff's plane about 30 feet off his wingtip, and Jeff smiling and waving at him, then giving him a thumb's up.

"Red One. Your plane doesn't look too bad from the outside. Some dents on your nose about where the hydraulic reservoir is located, but nothing is missing or in danger of falling off that I can see. What's your status? Over."

Matt described the damage to the windscreen and canopy as so bad that he couldn't see forward, bailout, or ditch. He then scanned the instrument panel and other gages and reported that the hydraulic pressure was zero – eliminating lowering the landing gear or flaps - and the engine temperature was high and rising.

Jeff took a moment to assess the situation and to come up with a plan, then radioed Matt.

"Red One, I think we need to demote you back to being my wingman. Then, you won't need to look forward; you're only supposed to watch me.

"We can get back to Wormingford safely together, flying in formation. We've already done it a hundred times.

"We'll both land side-by-side on the grass field between the runways. I'll let you know when you're close enough to the ground to flare.

"How's that sound, Red One? Over."

Matt considered the plan and thought it was great but then realized it had one major flaw.

"White One, that sounds like a great plan, with one exception. You're not landing gear and flaps up like me. You lower your gear and flaps on final, or I swear I'll nose-in. Nice try. Over."

Caught, Jeff tried lying,

"Red One, I swear I was going to lower my landing gear and flaps," but then sheepishly added, "You can remind me if I forget. OK? Over."

Matt shook his head back and forth, then smiled, replying,

"Roger, White One. It was before, is now, and always will be the honor of my life to be your wingman. Out," not caring who else might be listening.

Jeff contacted Wormingford's tower and advised them they were going to make an emergency landing, coming in from the southwest, in the field to the right of the main runway, and to have an emergency rescue crew ready to meet them.

The flight across the Channel was routine, but as Jeff lined them up with the main runway from two miles out, Matt's engine, whose gage had been displaying a red-lined temperature reading since the middle of the channel, suddenly seized.

"Red One to White One. My engine's quit. Doesn't look like I'm going to make the field. You go on ahead. I'll see you in a bit. Over."

"Negative, Red One. There's plenty of flat, green field ahead. These babies can glide forever. We'll get as close to home as we can before setting down. Over."

"Ok, White One. But remember your promise."

"I'm lowering my gear and flaps as we speak, Red One. See?"

Matt had pitched his nose over to maintain his airspeed above 100 mph, a little above the stall speed of the P-51. Jeff, with his landing gear and flaps lowered, was still able to stay alongside Matt by adjusting his engine and flight controls, though the plane's handling was mushy.

They were at 100 feet and within a half mile of the runway when Jeff decided that was as close as they could get. They were over farmland, clear of trees, with plenty of room ahead, when he thought they should set down. He decided to abandon radio etiquette.

"Matt, this looks like as good a place as any. I'm going to stay with you as long as I can.

"You need to touch down on your tail, keeping your nose high as long as possible, or your scoop is going to live up to its name and dig in, stopping you too quickly. Over."

"Roger, Jeff."

Then Jeff guided Matt down, saying, "You're at 50….40….30, start to flare….20, looking good…10..5..you're down!"

Both Matt and Jeff touched down alongside together, but Jeff quickly rolled past Matt, saying, "Matt, no worries, I'll be right back to get you out."

The landing was going smoother than Matt thought it would until the nose came down, and the scoop caught. The sudden deceleration forced Matt hard into the safety harness, bruising his shoulders and inner thighs.

Jeff landed safely but nearly tipped the plane over as he turned around at high speed, heading back to Matt.

As he neared Matt's plane, Jeff rolled the canopy back, killed the engine, unbuckled his harness, climbed out of the cockpit onto the port wing, and jumped from the wing before the plane came to a stop.

He raced to Matt's plane, ran around it to the right, starboard side, then climbed up the wing to the cockpit, where the outside emergency release button for the canopy was located.

When he pressed the release button, there was no resistance, like it had already been released.

He tried pulling and pushing on the canopy, but it wouldn't budge. Then he heard Matt screaming for him to get away: they both could smell gasoline leaking from one of the wing's internal fuel tanks that had ruptured.

Jeff could see the emergency vehicles racing to reach them but judged they were still too far away to rely on. So, Jeff climbed up onto the top of the canopy, sat on the top edge of the windscreen, facing rearward, and started frantically kicking the remains of the rearview mirror's base, bolted to the front edge of the canopy, as fast as he could and with all his might.

At first, the canopy didn't budge. But then a small gap, maybe a 1/16 of an inch, opened. With even more determination, Jeff continued to kick. All the while, Matt screamed for him to leave.

The gap continued to open until it was opened five inches, when Matt, still screaming, started punching Jeff's legs to get him to leave.

The emergency vehicles were still 30 seconds away when Jeff gave a final kick, sliding the canopy past the damaged section of tracks, then completely off its rails, with the canopy ending up leaning against the port side of the fuselage, aft of the wing.

Jeff jumped down onto the port wing and started helping Matt unbuckle his harness, then helped him out of the cockpit. They both jumped down off the wing together and ran away from the plane as fast as they could. They had barely gotten 100 feet away when the plane exploded, throwing them both to the ground, with Jeff's body partially shielding Matt from the blast.

They were lying on the ground catching their breath, watching the emergency crew arrive and start to put out the flames, when Matt, feeling unbelievable regret for nearly getting Jeff killed, said, "I'm so sorry, I'm such a mess."

Jeff, knowing how Matt was feeling, joked, "No, but your plane is. You know, Wes isn't going to give you your deposit back."

Matt didn't think anyone could ever make him smile again, but just then, Jeff did. Then Jeff added, smiling, "Any landing you can walk away from is a good one."

Thomas Willard © 2021

Everything seemed all right, and they were relaxing, waiting for the ambulance to pick them up when Matt noticed blood on his flight suit. He was surprised because he didn't think he was bleeding anywhere. Then, when he looked at Jeff to see if he was injured, he could see both of Jeff's hands were bleeding profusely through slits cut in his gloves.

Jeff had sliced through his gloves and cut both palms on the sharp edges of the canopy's rearview mirror when he'd tried pulling on it to pry the canopy open, but in the excitement, he hadn't noticed yet. What he did notice was a change in Matt's expression - to one of deep concern - and that he was crying.

Tears were pouring down Matt's face, but he didn't seem to realize it. His voice was steady and didn't match emotionally with his tears. Jeff thought Matt might have something in his eyes. So, he asked, "Matt, were you wearing your goggles? Do you have anything in your eyes?"

Matt said no, but had a questioning look on his face like it was a strange question for Jeff to ask.

#

EMOTIONAL SHOCK

The ambulance arrived and took Jeff to the dispensary, then delivered Matt to the Debriefing hut just two buildings away.

Matt, obviously concerned about Jeff and with tears still flowing, was distracted when answering questions. The pilots from Jeff's flight noticed and set up a relay to give Matt ongoing hand signals on how Jeff was doing: their signals were always thumbs up whenever Matt looked their way, whether they knew Jeff's status or not.

When Matt finished his debriefing, the interrogator, also concerned Matt might have something in his eyes or some other injury, ordered him to see Doc Garnett in the dispensary. Matt told him he was already planning on going there to check on Jeff and would ask to see Doc Garnett, too.

Doc Garnett, who was stitching Jeff's hand wounds, was called out of the treatment room by the nurse when she noticed Matt's tears.

The Doc, who had been briefed by Jeff on what had happened, looked at Matt's eyes but saw nothing obviously wrong and asked Matt if he'd been exposed to any chemicals or received a blow to the head.

Matt, totally unaware or unconcerned about his tears, said no, he'd been wearing his goggles during the collision and that the landing, though a little rough, hadn't resulted in any head trauma. And he said that he'd been shielded by Jeff from most of the blast from the explosion.

Doc Garnett noticed that Matt's voice was flat, showing no emotion in describing what would have been for anyone with a normal emotional response, a terrifying series of events.

When Doc Garnett went back into the treatment room to speak with Jeff, he told Jeff he was very concerned for Matt. He asked when Matt's tears had started. Jeff said they'd started right after Matt noticed Jeff's hands were bleeding.

Doc Garnet told Jeff he thought Matt could be suffering an emotional shock and that he might have to send Matt to a psychiatric hospital. Jeff begged him not to.

"Isn't there anything else that you can do?"

The Doc said, "I'm no psychiatrist. Normal protocol is to send someone who's been in a crash without injuries, like Matt, to the Flak house for rest, and someone like you, with injuries, to the hospital and then to the Flak house."

The Doc, seeing how dejected Jeff was, thought for a moment and had an idea.

"This may be a little humiliating for you."

Jeff said, "I don't care. I'll do anything."

So, the Doc explained his idea.

"I think Matt is suffering from guilt for getting you injured, for almost getting you killed in the explosion, and probably worst of all, for hitting you when he tried to get you to leave him.

"You're going to need 24-hour care for at least the next ten days, the kind of care you can only get in the hospital: the Flak house is not staffed to provide that kind of care.

"If you agree to let Matt take care of you like that at the Flak house, it might help him work off his guilt. The kind of care I'm talking about includes feeding, dressing, bathing, and even going to the bathroom. Are you up for that?"

The Doc knew Matt and Jeff were close but probably had some personal boundaries that hadn't been crossed. Could Jeff allow Matt to be that intimate with him? The Doc was also worried that Jeff was also emotionally damaged by the day's events. Would this be too much of a strain on him?

Jeff said, "I'm willing to do anything that might help Matt."

But then, the Doc started back peddling.

"I'm no Captain Spiegel. If he were here, I'd trust his judgment, but I'm not qualified to prescribe this treatment."

Jeff said, "What qualifies you is you know Matt and me as well, if not better than Captain Spiegel.

"We have ten days at the Flak house to get Matt well enough to pass a psych evaluation. If Matt doesn't improve by then, you can send him to a psych hospital, but I want to go with him: maybe I'm emotionally damaged, too. Anyway, I'm sure I can convince the visiting psychiatrist that I am."

The Doc, still worried, reluctantly agreed and said to help make their pitch to Matt more convincing, he was going to exaggerate Jeff's bandages. He didn't want Jeff to do anything with his hands for a while anyway, so the additional bandages would act to totally immobilize his hands and fingers. The Red Cross nurses at The Flak house would change his bandages every day and could reduce them once Matt had recovered.

Then the Doc said, "You need to get Matt to release his pent-up emotions, to get him to cry and wail it all out so that his emotions match his tears. It won't be an easy thing for you to see or hear. But just comfort him, don't try to stop him.

"When he gets it all out of him, tell one of the nurses to call me, day or night. I'll know then that Matt is emotionally healed,"

Thomas Willard © 2021

then he added, "You need to cry with him; it will help him to release, and you're probably in nearly as bad a shape as he is, so it would be good for you, too."

The Doc called Matt in and explained the plan for him to take care of Jeff at the Flak house, then asked if Matt was on board. Matt said he was more than certain he could do it; no worries.

So, the Doc said great, but then added, "Jeff just mentioned he needs to use the restroom. Would you take him there and give him a hand?"

Jeff, a little shocked and a bit miffed the Doc was testing him like this, reluctantly asked, "Yeah, Matt, could you help me?"

Matt nodded yes, then brought Jeff to the restroom.

Matt took them both into a stall and shut the door. They were both in their flight suits, so it was going to take a little effort to free their penises.

To ease Jeff's embarrassment, Matt raised the zipper of his own flight suit first – the two-way zipper both raised from the bottom and lowered from the top - unzipped his pants, then reached through the flaps of his long johns and his boxers to fish out his penis and relieved himself.

Jeff thought, "Matt is barely hanging on emotionally; he rammed a plane, crash landed, came within 15 seconds of getting blown up, and is worried about embarrassing me." Jeff resolved then not to be embarrassed no matter what Matt had to do for him.

Matt, leaving himself exposed, repeated the undressing process on Jeff, then aimed his penis at the bowl. Jeff, who had worried about pee-shyness, once he was all out there, let loose. When he finished, Matt shook him several times until there was no dripping, then carefully put Jeff's penis back into his underwear and pants, then zipped his flight suit back down. Then, he did the same to himself.

They paused at the sink for Matt to wash his hands, then went back to the treatment room.

The Doc asked Matt to wait outside while he finished wrapping Jeff's bandages. When Matt was gone, the Doc asked, "How did it go?"

Jeff said, "Better than I could ever have imagined. Matt has to be the most considerate person in the world. He tried to preserve as much of my dignity as possible."

Then the Doc asked, "Did you notice anything different about him?"

Jeff said, "No, not really. But I was feeling a little embarrassed and had trouble looking him in the eye."

Then the Doc said, with obvious relief in his voice, "He's stopped crying."

CHAPTER 5 — STANBRIDGE EARLS REVISITED: 11-21

SEPTEMBER 1944

ALL-HANDS

When Jeff emerged from the treatment room, his hands were bandaged so much it looked like he was wearing a pair of white boxing gloves. He thought the Doc had gone more than a little overboard on the bandages – they were embarrassing – but it was worth it when he saw they had the desired effect on Matt.

Matt, who normally would have been teasing Jeff about how ridiculous he looked, instead, was all business. He had a purpose now: to take care of Jeff, reinforced by Doc Garnett, who

said, before releasing them to get ready for the trip to the Flak
house,

"Matt, I'm placing Jeff in your charge. I'm trusting you to
keep him from using his hands in any way, no matter how much he
whines about it.

"If you have any trouble with him – if he doesn't want you
to feed or bathe him, or whatever – let me know. I won't bother the
Red Cross nurses, but there's a woman there, a Mrs. Frobisher, the
baker, that's worked in a nursing home before, and she'll be more
than glad to help you," then smiled and thought to himself, "More
than glad."

The Doc had provided his staff car and driver to take Matt
and Jeff to the Flak house, but first, they needed to stop at the
Ready Room to change out of their flight gear and into their
regular uniforms.

Again, Matt stripped down first to just his boxers, t-shirt,
and socks before helping Jeff remove his flight gear. When he saw
he wouldn't be able to get Jeff's hands past the sleeves of Jeff's

flight suit or thermal underwear, Matt quickly and without asking used his survival knife to cut the sleeves of both enough to easily slide over the bandages. He examined the cuffs of the shirt and, unbuttoned, judged they would fit over the bandages, which they did.

Jeff wasn't offended by Matt's not asking permission. He knew Matt well by the - that he became non-verbal when he was extremely upset. But Jeff had learned how to communicate with him then anyway, by listening to his grunts and observing his body language and by continuing to speak to him as though Matt was contributing to the conversation because if you listened carefully enough, he was.

After Matt finished stripping Jeff down, he began dressing him, starting with his pants. He finished dressing Jeff, then tied his tie before dressing himself.

They picked up their personal belongings from the Intelligence Officer, then returned to the staff car for the nearly three-hour drive to Stanbridge Earls.

The drive was relaxing after what they'd been through, and Jeff almost immediately fell asleep, using Matt as a pillow. Matt, though, still on high alert, didn't sleep a wink.

They arrived at the Manor around 2030, an hour and a half after dinner. But the staff had been warned they'd be coming late and had left them a tray with chicken sandwiches, tea, and apple pie in their room, the same double room they'd had before, though a small table and two chairs had been added so they could take their meals in their room, saving Jeff the embarrassment of being fed in public.

After they had settled in and visited the bathroom, Jeff said he was starving, so they sat down to eat.

Matt, who Jeff realized hadn't spoken since the dispensary, began quietly feeding Jeff.

Jeff quickly caught on that Matt wasn't eating, so he decided to push both issues and said.

"I'm not eating if you don't."

Matt, who wasn't hungry, but absorbed with the task of feeding Jeff, thought he'd heard Jeff make a bargain with him: if he ate, Jeff would eat. So, Matt grabbed a half sandwich and took a bite. Then he offered the same sandwich to Jeff.

Jeff thought, "Problem number one solved; on to number two." He stretched his legs out and encircled Matt's, pressing his legs into Matt's, making as much contact with him as he could. Then said,

"You have to talk to me too, or no deal."

Matt, totally committed to his feeding mission, thought he heard another bargain being made. So, he took another bite of the sandwich – it was his turn – swallowed, and asked,

"What do you want to talk about?"

Jeff smiled and said,

"Anything you want. I just like the sound of your voice."

That opened things up. Together, they devoured the meal. And they talked about what they'd do while they were there, all the places they had missed seeing before. But the tacit agreement between them was absolutely nothing about that day's flight.

Once they'd finished eating, they were tired and ready for bed. There was a note asking them to leave the tray outside their door when they'd finished, which Matt did. Then Matt stripped down to his underwear and then stripped Jeff down, too.

Matt turned the two beds down, then helped Jeff into his and covered him with the sheet and blanket before turning off the light and crawling into his own bed.

After they both said goodnight, the room fell quiet. Jeff was about to fall asleep when he heard the muffled sound of Matt trying to stifle his crying. Not wanting to point out he knew Matt was crying, Jeff asked Matt for a favor.

"Matt, are you still awake? I can't sleep with these bandages. Do you think you could give me a backrub?"

Matt, now with another mission, was up like a shot.

Jeff said, "Lock the door while you're up," and then made room for Matt.

Matt crawled into bed with Jeff, then, with Jeff facing away, his back towards him, began rubbing Jeff's back, first over his t-shirt, then with his hand underneath the shirt, rubbing his bare skin.

After a few minutes, Jeff said, "That feels great; I'm almost asleep. You'll need to hold me for a while first."

Matt scooted close to Jeff and wrapped his arms around him, holding him close. Jeff thought too close; he could hardly breathe. But then he felt Matt begin to relax his hold, breathe easier, and, finally succumbing to total exhaustion, fall asleep.

When Jeff heard Matt gently snoring in his ear, he thought, "That's good. Problem number three down," before falling asleep himself.

They woke up early the next morning and decided to take a shower before breakfast and before any of the other guests were awake.

Matt helped Jeff into a bathrobe and slippers, and then himself, then headed them for the bathroom on the same floor just two doors down.

Once inside, Matt removed their bathrobes but kept going and stripped, first himself, then Jeff, bare. Following his practice of always humiliating himself first, Matt sat on the commode to do his business, then had Jeff do the same. Jeff, who'd been dreading this last indignity, found the experience, because of Matt, not much worse than in the common latrine area on the base, where there really wasn't that much more privacy.

Matt started the shower and adjusted the temperature, and then helped Jeff in. He quickly shampooed and washed himself before starting on Jeff. He'd just finished shampooing Jeff and had started washing his back when Mrs. Frobisher, who had been alerted by Doc Garnett through one of the Red Cross nurses that she might be needed to help Matt with Jeff, walked in with a stack of towels, getting a full-frontal view of Jeff through the half-opened shower curtain.

Jeff sheepishly said, "Hello, Mrs. Frobisher. We'll just be a couple of more minutes."

After she left, when they were out of the shower and while Jeff was being dried, Matt - who had been shielded from view by Jeff – totally lost it and began laughing hysterically. He laid down on the floor in the fetal position and was laughing so hard he could hardly breathe.

Jeff, at first, was glad that Matt was laughing so hard; maybe it would help. But when Matt didn't stop, he worried that it was a sign of repressed sadness. So, trying to get Matt back in self-control reminded him, "You know I like to keep things even."

Matt, suddenly terrified, assumed Jeff was plotting to expose him to Mrs. Frobisher and sobered up quickly.

#

DARE BACKFIRE

Thomas Willard © 2021

For the rest of the day, Matt was an emotional wreck. He'd taken Jeff's taunt too seriously and had blown it way out of proportion. Jeff tried to tell him he was just teasing, but Matt became more and more convinced that Jeff meant to make good on his threat to get even.

Jeff was worried by Matt's increasingly wild mood swings and knew they were out of character. Matt was getting worse, not better. He blamed himself; for his taunt.

By dinner, Jeff knew something had to be done: Matt was becoming irrational. Every time Mrs. Frobisher got within 50 feet of them, Matt showed signs of panic, like he expected Jeff to strip him in front of her, forgetting that it would be impossible with his hands practically in oven mitts.

So, Jeff devised a plan and asked one of the Red Cross nurses for help. Did she know of a pub in Romsey that had a piano? She said yes, the Tudor Rose, that it was within walking distance, and gave him directions.

After dinner in their room, Jeff told Matt he wanted to go to Romsey for a beer and asked if he would take him there. A little paranoid now, Matt said yes, but then asked if they would be going alone. Jeff said it would be just the two of them and that he'd like to get started soon while it was still light out.

Once they were away from the Manor, and Mrs. Frobisher, Matt started to relax. Jeff, sensing a change, thought he'd try to calm Matt down further.

"You know I love you, Matt. I would never do anything to hurt you.

"As far as exposing you to Mrs. Frobisher goes, first, that wasn't your fault. You had nothing to do with it, so why would exposing you to her even things up?

"And second, I'd never expose you that way to anyone. I'm the only one that gets to see you like that, except for the guys in the barrack's showers, but they don't care about you that way, so they don't count."

"I'm glad it was me and not you that she saw. I'd be really pissed off at her otherwise and would never forgive her. She can look at me all she wants, but if she ever walks in on purpose again and sees you…." Jeff, a little choked up, couldn't finish the sentence. He was just as hyper-protective of Matt as ever, maybe more so after the events of the day before.

Matt, still not himself or processing things correctly, felt a sudden need to hug Jeff - that Jeff needed him then and that Jeff, with his hands bandaged, couldn't hug him like he wanted to.

Matt didn't care where they were or who could see them. He thought Jeff needed to know that Matt loved him just as much. So, he turned to face Jeff, wrapped his arms around him, and hugged him as hard as he could. Matt said, "I love you so much. And I know you'd never hurt me.

"I'm not myself for some reason; I'm losing my perspective and blowing the smallest things out of proportion.

"I don't care if Mrs. Frobisher sees me or not. Normally, I'd think it was kind of funny, so don't stress about protecting me from her.

"I don't know why I'm making such a big deal out of it. Let's go back right now; I'll give her a show. She's earned it: she makes a great apple pie." Then he added, "I noticed she gave you an extra-large slice of pie for dinner: a sign of appreciation, I bet. She has very good taste."

Jeff, astonished at Matt's sudden return to lucidity, was still worried. Matt's mood was swinging all over the place. Was this just a temporary change back to normal? He thought Matt was either on the verge of a breakthrough or a total meltdown. The psych evaluation could come at any time, so he needed to find out which direction Matt's mental state was headed, and soon.

"No way you're going back to give her a show. Any show like that is only for me.

"Let's keep walking to town. There's a pub there, the Tudor Rose, I'd like to check out."

When they'd reached the town's center and were outside the pub, about to go in, Jeff thought he'd try to eliminate the damage his "keeping things even" taunt that morning had done by replacing it with a minimally-embarrassing substitute.

Jeff said, "I've created a monster with this 'keeping things even" crap. It's a private joke between us that's gotten way out of hand. I don't keep score like that.

"I know most of you isn't worried about it anymore, but for the little bit of you that still is, I've got a small dare to even things up. It might be a little humiliating – it would have to be, I guess - but I promise none of your clothes will come off. Deal?"

Matt had already relapsed a little, but not enough for Jeff to notice yet. Not sure what the right emotional response was to being dared, Matt took what seemed to him as the path of least resistance and said, "Deal."

The Tudor Rose is a small, no-frills pub in the center of Romsey that, on a good day, can hold at most 25 people if the fire marshal is looking the other way. Its history was lost until remodeling in 1928 revealed it was built in the 15th century and is probably the oldest pub in Romsey. It has two red-painted doors, one at each end of the building, both facing the street and is made of massive oak timbers. There's a bar along the sidewall at one end and a large fireplace and dart board on the wall at the opposite end, with wooden benches and chairs loosely arranged in between.

Matt and Jeff entered the door closest to the bar, which was to their left. To their right, just beyond the door, they saw an up-right piano backed up against the front wall. There were only a few people – who looked to be older, local regulars - in the bar, which is what Jeff had hoped for, the reason he'd rushed Matt to get them there early: he wanted as few people as possible to witness Matt's embarrassment.

They approached the bartender, a burly man in his late forties that might have once been in the navy or merchant marines judging by the tattoos on his forearms, and ordered two beers, one with a straw.

When they'd nearly finished their beer, Jeff, in a whispered, conspiratorial tone, said,

"Ok, Matt, here's the dare. You're going to get us kicked out of here.

"You've been twenty-one for over two months now and haven't been kicked out of a bar yet, so you're way overdue."

Matt, wishing he'd asked what the dare was before they came in there, didn't have a clue how to get kicked out of a bar. So, he asked Jeff,

"How do I do that? Do I have to pick a fight? These people seem nice, and it's their bar; we're guests. I don't want to be rude."

Jeff smiled and said, "No, nothing like that. You just have to play a song on the piano for a second. The bartender doesn't look like he has a sense of humor. He'll throw us the hell out of here in no time."

Matt asked, "How do I do this; what do I play?"

Jeff said, "I'll ask the bartender if you can play a song. If he says no, the dare is over, and we're even. If he says yes, you have to play a song, any song. Play "Chopsticks"; everyone knows how to play that. OK?"

Matt reluctantly nodded yes. Jeff called the bartender over and asked if his friend, pointing at Matt, could play a song. The bartender, a little wary, tired of being pranked by the Yanks from the Manor up the road, looked at Jeff's bandages, then said sure but warned no funny business or drinks near the piano.

Jeff nodded to Matt in the direction of the piano. As soon as Matt began walking to the piano, an unruly mob of customers, mostly pilots from the Manor - some from their Group - who'd been bar-hopping, entered the door at the far end. They recognized Matt, now seated at the piano, and Jeff at the bar and started hooting for Matt to play.

Jeff frantically yelled, "Abort, Matt. We're even!"

The bartender, who now realized he'd been had and was even questioning whether the bandages on Jeff's hands were real, grabbed and lifted Jeff by the front of his shirt and, in Jeff's face, menacingly asked, "What are you two trying to pull?"

When he saw Jeff wince, bracing for the bartender to punch him, Matt played the first three notes of probably the then most recognizable song in England, "The White Cliffs of Dover."

The song, written in 1941, when Britain was fighting the Germans alone, and the outcome of the war was far from certain, was more a furtive hope for better days to come than a proud anthem.

Matt played the song softly, without flourish, but with a lot of emotion. He beautifully captured all the sadness and longing, but also the wistful hope, in the song.

Early into the song, the rowdy crowd had hushed, mesmerized by Matt's playing. The bartender, who was born and raised near Dover, and had been bombed in London during the Blitz, quickly released Jeff and was now unabashedly sobbing.

Jeff was also crying and thunderstruck. Shaking his head in amazement, he thought, "Well, this dare backfired big time. I should have asked if he could play the piano." Then, in admiration, he thought, " Is there anything this guy can't do?"

As Matt finished playing, he used the sustain pedal on the last note, which hung in the air over the deathly-quiet crowd for five seconds before they erupted with cheers and applause.

The bartender, still blubbering, was all apologies. But though the crowd was cheering wildly, Jeff noticed Matt wasn't acknowledging them. He looked stunned like he'd been in a trance playing the song and was now stuck, unable to come out of it.

Jeff was worried Matt might be about to have a breakdown now, here, in public. So, he quickly made his way to Matt before the crowd decided to rush him.

Putting his arm around Matt's shoulder, Jeff said,

"Hey, Matt. Good song choice; I think you saved me from a broken nose. But I thought you were going to play "Chopsticks." You had the bartender crying like a baby. Me, too."

Then joked, "Just for the record, is there anything you can't do?"

Matt smiled and seemed to be coming out of his fog a little. Then said, "I can't dance, but I'm working on it. I have a hell of a teacher."

Jeff asked, seriously this time, with concern,

"How are you doing? That was a beautiful song but a bit sad. Did it get to you a little?"

Matt nodded yes. Jeff, thinking Matt needed a little more time to recover and to lighten Matt's mood, gestured to the bartender for permission for them to do one more song.

Jeff asked, "How about we try one together? Do you know "They'll Be Some Changes Made," the upbeat tempo version, like Count Basie's?"

Matt said, "Yes, I think so. My dad's the real piano player in the family; I'm just a hack. That's one of his favorites, so I've heard him play it a lot. I've never played it before, though. Do you know what key you want it in?"

Jeff smiled, like he even knew what key choices were, and said, "No, but no worries. You make up the music, and I'll make up the words. Something tells me none of these guys went to Julliard, so they won't know the difference. You know how to play a vamp, right?"

Matt nodded yes, then Jeff, still smiling, said, "Of course you do," as he mussed Matt's hair.

Jeff said, "Here we go. I'll warn you when I think you should improvise a little."

Matt thought, "Improvise a little? I hope I can remember five notes of this song."

Jeff counted the beat, "Bom...Bom... Bom," to get them started, and they were off.

"There'll be a change in the weather, a change in the sea.

From now on, there'll be a change in me.

My walk will be different, my talk, and my name.

Ain't nothin' about me's gonna be the same.

I'm gonna change my way of livin', and if that ain't
enough,

I'll even change the way I strut my stuff.

'Cause nobody wants you when you're old and gray.

There'll be some changes made starting today.

There'll be some changes made."

Pointing his bandaged right hand at Matt, Jeff said, "Ah, let's hear the band," and Matt played a solo chorus to wild applause. Then Jeff resumed singing.

"My walk will be different, my talk, and my name,

Ain't nothin' about me's gonna be the same."

Jeff said, "All right," as Matt played a second solo chorus, then he continued,

"Nobody wants you when you're old and gray.

There'll be some changes made startin' today.

There'll be some changes made.

Change in the weather don't mean a thing; from this day forth, every day will swing.

Change in tide that's in the sea, there's gonna be a change in me.

My walk will be different; it'll be slightly insane.

Ain't nothin' about me's gonna be the same.

I'm gonna change my way of livin', baby; you better start'n changing, too.

Have your fling and start to swing; before your swinging days are through,

> *'Cause nobody wants you when you're old and gray.*
>
> *There'll be some changes made today.*
>
> *Out with the old stuff, in with the new stuff,*
>
> *There'll be a lot of changes made.*
>
> *Don't want no sad songs, just sing me glad songs,*
>
> *There'll be a lot of changes made.*
>
> *Gonna get a new look, gonna read a new book,*
>
> *You know there'll be some changes made."*

Jeff, who normally sang tenor, switched to baritone for the last stanza, lowering the register an octave and ending on a deep bass note. Matt played the final three notes as Jeff held the bass note, then finished with a glissando slide.

The crowd immediately burst into cheering and wild applause led by the bartender. Jeff looked out over the crowd and exclaimed, "And the crowd goes wild!!" Then he pointed to Matt and said, "Let's hear it for the band. He's unbelievable," as he cheered Matt with the crowd, shaking his head in wonder.

Matt was beaming, happy he'd made Jeff so happy. Jeff asked him, "We're even, right?" When Matt nodded yes, Jeff said, "Good, because we're done keeping things even. Never again, I'm sorry. OK?"

Matt nodded in agreement again. Then Jeff, in a gentle voice, asked, "How are you doing; are you OK?"

Matt, now in a much better mood, said, "Yes, but I'm still a little wobbly."

Jeff bent over and said, "That's OK. Just wrap your arms around my neck, and I'll help you up." Then, when they were both standing said, "What do you say, let's get out of here," and headed them for the door, waving goodbye to the crowd, ignoring their calls for another song.

Once outside in the fresh air, Matt recovered quickly and no longer needed Jeff's assistance to walk. But Jeff kept his arm around Matt's shoulder anyway, just to keep him close.

To keep the mood light, Jeff said, "You're really a great piano player. I think if we go back there tomorrow night, we'll make five bucks in tips. Or at least we'll get free beer from the bartender; he loves you."

Jeff was trying hard not to show it, but he was now deeply concerned about Matt's rapid mood swings and thought they were a sign that Matt was becoming emotionally unstable.

Matt was feeling great, animated, playful, and almost giddy. For some reason, Jeff's last bass note had tickled him, and he kept getting Jeff to repeat it. Jeff always obliged, trying to keep Matt in a good mood until they could reach a safe, secluded place.

#

DUCK POND PURGE

As they got closer to the Manor, Jeff worried that Matt might have another Frobisher-panic attack, but when he didn't, Jeff accepted that Matt was truly over that issue; somehow, his crazy dare scheme had worked.

Jeff walked them past the main entrance to the Manor, saying, "It's nice out tonight. Do you mind if we stay outside for a while?" and headed them towards the far side of the duck pond in front of the Manor.

When they'd reached a dark, secluded grassy spot well out of ear-shot of the Manor that gently sloped downward, they laid down a few feet from the water, looking out over the pond.

Jeff began, "Matt, I'm so frustrated I can't touch you with these bandages on; I'm going crazy. Could you do me a favor? Take my shoes and socks off, and yours, too."

When Matt had finished removing their shoes and socks, Jeff instantly began rubbing his bare feet all over Matt's, relieving some of his pent-up need.

"Thanks, that helped a lot. But it's not enough. I need you to do something else. I want you to remove the outer layer of bandages from my hands, enough so my fingertips are free to touch you."

Matt balked, worried that he'd be violating Doc Garnett's trust in him and that he'd be risking injuring Jeff.

"I can't; I'm not supposed to. Please don't make me. I don't want to hurt you."

Jeff was caught in a Catch-22 inadvertently created by Doc Garnett: he couldn't help Matt experience a breakthrough without touching him, but his bandages couldn't come off until Matt had a breakthrough.

"I'll be all right, I swear. The outer bandages are supposed to come off tomorrow morning anyway. I just really need to touch you now, tonight."

When he saw Matt wouldn't budge, he said, "Ok, I'll have to take them off myself," and started gnawing on the bandage on his right hand.

Matt, in a panic, said, "No, you can't. You'll mess them all up and get them wet."

Jeff said, "Well then, help me do it right. I only want to remove the outer layer. Remember, you took me to the bathroom on base before the outer layer was added, and it was fine. I won't get infected. And I won't try to use my hands; you'll still have to do everything for me. But I have to be able to touch you now. It's important."

Matt, whose mood had suddenly switched back to sad, began unwrapping Jeff's hands.

When his fingers were free, Jeff said, "Thank you. That's much better. Now, lay your head down on my chest; I want to talk to you."

Matt laid his head on Jeff's chest, and Jeff began stroking his hair. They were quiet for a few minutes while Jeff collected his thoughts and comforted Matt.

"Matt, you know I would never lie or try to hurt you. I care so much about you; it hurts sometimes. And now is one of those times.

"I know you don't want to talk about the mission, but we have to. Something happened to you after the mission.

"You didn't seem to notice, but you were crying just before the ambulance picked us up and all through debriefing. Everyone else noticed, especially Doc Garnett. He thinks you experienced an emotional shock and were having a breakdown. He wanted to send you to a psychiatric hospital, but I begged him not to, that I could help you here.

"Since we got here, though, you've been having large, sudden mood swings. You've noticed yourself; you said so tonight.

"Maybe you'll get better on your own by the end of our stay. But your mood swings are getting worse, and your psych evaluation could happen any day.

"Doc Garnett only agreed to let me take you here if I promised to get you to talk about what happened to upset you so much and to cry it all out.

"I think Captain Spiegel and now Doc Garnett have figured us both out. We're the cause and the cure to any severe emotional problem either of us is having.

"Spiegel knew the secret of saving you was for you to save me. The Doc used the same logic to get you to stop crying by letting you help me.

"I think they are right about us: if you're upset, I'm the cause. But that means I'm also somehow the solution. I'll do anything to save you, so we just need to figure out what I've done to upset you, and I'll change it. Then we'll both have a good cry, and we'll be done."

That seemed like a straightforward solution, but when Jeff asked Matt to tell him what was bothering him, Matt drew a blank, then acted like he didn't want to think about it anymore and tried to be playful instead, rubbing his feet with Jeff's.

Jeff realized he had put the cart before the horse, that Doc Garnett was right about the sequence of events: they needed to cry first before they could talk. So, Jeff switched tactics.

"I liked the first song you played, "The White Cliffs of Dover," a lot. I wished you had sung it. I think I know how it goes." Then, in a whisper and into Matt's ear, he started to sing.

"They'll be blue birds over,

The white cliffs of Dover,

Tomorrow, just you wait and see.

Matt stirred and said, "No, Jeff, please don't sing that song. It'll make me unhappy; I don't want to be unhappy." But Jeff kept going anyway.

"There'll be love and laughter,

And peace ever after

Tomorrow, when the world is free.

"Stop, please. Why are you trying to make me cry?"

The shepherd will tend his sheep,

The valley will bloom again,

And Jimmy will go to sleep,

In his own little room again."

Matt was softly crying now, and Jeff was holding him with one hand and gently stroking his hair with the other while he continued to sing.

"There'll be bluebirds over,"

Then suddenly, Matt let out his first wail, so loud Jeff was shaken, but kept singing, his voice cracking as he began losing control himself.

"The white cliffs of Dover,

Tomorrow, just you wait and see."

Matt was sobbing uncontrollably and wailing; Jeff had opened the floodgates. Pained by hearing Matt in such agony, all he could do was hold Matt closer and tell him, "That's it. Let it all out. There's nobody here. It's just you, me, and the ducks."

Matt began retching, alternating between vomiting violently and wailing and sobbing. Jeff was crying, too, out of sympathy for Matt but also to let some of his own emotions out.

Jeff continued to hold and comfort Matt, letting him purge himself of all his emotional pain while Jeff softly cried along with him.

Finally, after more than an hour, Matt's retching and wailing stopped, but he was still sobbing. Jeff sensed Matt might have reached the point where he'd be able to talk about his feelings, about why he was so upset.

Jeff had spent the time thinking about what the reason might be and decided to share his thoughts with Matt to get him started.

"I think you might be mad at me because I wouldn't go away when you told me to after the crash. In the same way that I was mad at you for almost getting killed saving the bomber.

"We weren't really mad; we were just scared for each other.

"My heart was in my throat when I saw you zoom-climb. Your plane was turned so that I had a broad view of your wings. I thought it would be the last time I ever saw you."

Matt, trying to talk while sobbing, said, "You wouldn't leave. I told you to leave, and you wouldn't leave. You were nearly blown up."

"I'd never leave you like that, Matt, no matter how mad you got at me. And you wouldn't have left me, either, so don't pretend you would have." Then, trying a little humor, added, "I don't think I would have hit you, though, to get you to leave."

That unintentionally struck a nerve, and Matt let out another wail. "I was hitting you. Me, hitting you, and you were bleeding," then Matt wailed again.

Jeff said tenderly, "It's OK to get angry at me; I deserve it sometimes, probably all the time. And I didn't feel you hitting me that much. We have to work on your punching."

Then, finally realizing what might have been bothering Matt the most all along, Jeff said,

"You know, you can be mad at someone and still love them. I love you so much, and I never for a second thought you didn't love me," getting a big smooch from a runny-nosed Matt in return, who took another hour to cry himself out before falling asleep on top of Jeff.

BACK TO NORMAL

Matt was sleeping peacefully, lightly snoring while Jeff was still stroking Matt's hair and gently rubbing his back with his thumb. He wished he could let him sleep there all night, but it was getting close to the midnight curfew when everyone had to be back at the Manor.

Gently shaking Matt, Jeff said, " Hey, guy, it's getting late. We have to get back."

Matt gradually awoke. He felt refreshed like the weight of the world had been lifted from his shoulders. He kissed Jeff, then said,

"Thanks, Jeff. I'm good now. You've saved me again."

Something in Matt's voice, maybe it was its strength and confidence, told Jeff it was true. They stood up and hugged each other. Jeff said,

"Thank God. I was scared, so scared."

Matt grabbed their shoes and socks and, together, with their arm over each other's shoulder, walked barefoot back to the main entrance to the Manor.

Once inside, Jeff said,

"I promised to let Doc Garnett know, day or night, when you were better," as he led them to the Red Cross nurses' room.

Jeff knocked on the door, and one of the nurses answered. Jeff said,

"Sorry to bother you so late. Could you please tell Doc Garnett thank you for us and that he can relax, that everything's good now? And let him know that we said he is as good as Captain Spiegel."

They went up to their room, and Matt undressed them down to their underwear. Then he put on their bathrobes and slippers, grabbed their ditty bags, and visited the bathroom.

They relieved themselves together, something that by then had become routine. Then Matt brushed their teeth, starting with his own, then Jeff's. Jeff noticed a confidence, but still a tenderness, in the way Matt maneuvered him around when he was brushing his teeth that wasn't there before. Matt seemed very comfortable helping Jeff like he was no longer invading Jeff's personal space but belonged there. Jeff really liked the change.

They went back to their room, and Matt turned down Jeff's bed, but not his own. He removed their bathrobes and slippers, then helped Jeff into his bed. He locked the door, got into bed with Jeff - the first time ever without waiting to be asked - and turned out the light before snuggling up to Jeff. He put an arm around Jeff, stroked his hair, then said,

"Jeff, I love you more than I can say. You're an amazing person; I hope you know that. I'm the luckiest guy in the world," all without tearing up or with a catch in his throat, another first.

The same couldn't be said for Jeff, who had tears of joy in his eyes but was left wondering who this guy next to him in bed was and what had he done with the real Matt? Completely exhausted, they were both sound asleep in minutes.

The next morning, they were up early again to enjoy the luxury of being able to shower every day – unlike on base, where they could only shower once a week.

Jeff again was surprised by Matt's confident, open attitude towards him. He was more playful and gave as good as he got. Matt stripped them down and got them into the shower but took every opportunity to grope Jeff that he could. The result was they were both sporting erections when they heard a knock on the door, then Mrs. Frobisher enter.

They were expecting her this time and were prepared. Matt asked Jeff, "Ready?" and then opened the curtain, exposing them both. But this time, there was a lot more of them to see. In unison, they said, " Good morning, Mrs. Frobisher. Thank you." Mrs. Frobisher smiled, put the towels on the vanity, and left, leaving a laughing pair of naked pilots in her wake. Later that evening, they would be rewarded with nearly half an apple pie each for dinner.

When they returned to their room after the shower, Matt removed their bathrobes and slippers, but instead of dressing them, he removed their t-shirts as well.

He said to Jeff, "You look tired to me," and gently pushed him down on the bed.

Matt laid down next to him, but with his head at Jeff's feet. "Last night, when we were rubbing our feet together, I thought I noticed something," as he reached over to touch Jeff's foot. Jeff, whose feet Matt had discovered were ticklish, protested, saying, "No. I'm ticklish. Stop," then added, "It's not fair; I'm defenseless," while trying to squirm away.

Matt, smiling, said, "I find that hard to believe.

"You're always telling me I have a magic touch. Well, let's see.

"Trust me; I promise I won't try to tickle you."

Matt held Jeff's foot to desensitize him a little. Then he rubbed the sole of the foot hard with his thumb and fingers, trying to avoid any tickling sensation. When he felt Jeff relax and then heard him let out a groan, he knew he was on to something. He massaged one foot for twenty minutes, then switched to the other. As Jeff's body began to trust him, Matt found he could lighten the pressure quite a bit and just rub normally without triggering any tickling reflex.

Jeff was totally relaxed. He'd even put his arms above his head, completely exposing his other ticklish area, his armpits, without realizing it.

"That's so amazing, Matt. I'm in heaven."

Matt noticed that Jeff was relaxed everywhere except one obvious area that was now pointing skyward, straining at his one remaining article of clothing.

Matt shifted up to Jeff's hips, then put his thumbs under the elastic band on either side of Jeff's boxers and slowly pulled them down, saying, "You don't need these," as Jeff lifted his butt so Matt could more easily remove them.

Once Jeff was naked, Matt positioned himself near Jeff's knees and began rubbing Jeff's feet and stroking Jeff's penis.

Jeff's testicles had already risen, and his penis was leaking precum, so Matt knew it wouldn't be long. Sure enough, less than two minutes after being stripped, Jeff exploded, with the first volley hitting his chin, followed by four nearly equally forceful shots.

Matt cleaned Jeff with a damp towel from the shower, then laid with his head next to Jeff's and tenderly kissed him. As he was starting to recover, Jeff tried to reach for Matt to return the favor, but Matt said, "Nope, you said we don't have to keep things even anymore. This is all about you. You deserve it; just relax. I put you through hell these past few days."

Matt turned down Jeff's covers, saying, "You usually take a nap afterward, but I need to cover you first, or I'll be perving on you the whole time you're asleep."

Jeff said, "You'll be perving on me? You and Mrs. Frobisher, who knew? That was pretty gutsy of you in the shower, by the way; I'm proud of you."

Smiling, Matt replied, "Not really. I knew she'd mostly be looking at you anyway. I would if I were her." Then Matt gently rubbed Jeff's back until they both fell asleep.

CHAPTER 6 — COMPLETING SECOND TOUR-OF-DUTY:

MID-SEPTEMBER 1944 TO MID-FEBRUARY 1945

RETURN TO DUTY

When their ten-day stay at the Flak house was up, Matt and Jeff

took the shuttle bus sent to retrieve them, along with several other

55th Fighter Group pilots, to return to base.

They had just gotten to their barracks when the Group's

adjutant arrived and asked them to report to Colonel Crowell's

office as soon as they were settled.

When they were outside the Colonel's office door,

preparing to enter and snap-salute to report for duty, the door opened, and Colonel Crowell came out, extending his hand to Matt to welcome them.

He invited them into his office, where two other officers were waiting for them. Colonel Crowell came right to the point.

"Matt, this is First Lieutenant James Watkins. He's from the 100th Bomb Group, 349th Bomb Squadron.

"And Jeff, this is First Lieutenant Joseph Husvar from our own 2015th Engineer Aviation Fire Fighting Platoon.

"These men are here to witness what normally is a very public ceremony, usually presided over by the theater commander. But, in deference to one of you, I've requested and been awarded the privilege of presenting these medals myself, here, in private.

"For exceptional valor, gallantry, and heroism in the face of great danger and personal risk, it is my honor to award you both with the Silver Star. You two are Aces now, credited with five kills after your last mission, so you are doubly eligible.

"Lieutenant Watkins was the pilot of the B-17 you saved, Matt. He's been relentless, calling every day since the Ruhland mission to see how you were doing. He's the one that recommended you for the metal.

"Lieutenant Husvar was leading the firefighting platoon, Jeff, desperately trying to reach Matt's plane in time. He watched as you frantically tried to rescue Matt, with the two of you barely escaping with your lives. He's the one that recommended you for the metal."

With that, the Colonel pinned the medals on Matt and Jeff, and then the three witnessing officers came to attention and saluted Matt and Jeff, who quickly returned their salutes. Then Colonel shook Matt's hand again before dismissing all of them.

Once outside the Colonel's office, Lieutenants Watkins and Husvar shook Matt's hand, then congratulated both Matt and Jeff before asking if they could buy them a beer at the Officers Club to celebrate. Matt and Jeff agreed, but only if they could buy a round, too.

When everyone had left his office, and he heard Matt and Jeff arrange to meet the two-witnessing officers at the Officers Club to celebrate, Colonel Crowell took a moment to reflect.

The USAAF had been revising its pilot evaluation criteria based on feedback on combat productivity. They found that their criteria accurately predicted what Air Cadets would successfully make it through flight training, but it did not predict what fighter pilots would be the most productive in combat.

When the Air Force reviewed the combat data, it found that five percent of fighter pilots accounted for 95 percent of the kills. Whether this was due to luck or not - being at the right place and at the right time - couldn't be determined. Surprisingly, though, it found that an aggressive-personality type did not correlate with productiveness in combat. In fact, the opposite was true: it was often the quiet, contemplative ones that were the most productive, making up a large percentage of the five percent-most productive fighter pilots.

Colonel Crowell, considering Matt, as well as several other of his pilots that had a similar quiet nature, had now come to fully endorse this conclusion.

#

BATTLE OF THE BULGE: 16 DECEMBER 1944 TO 25 JANUARY 1945

For most of the fall - through October and November – the Allies continued to pound Germany, especially its cities and were decimating the weakening Luftwaffe.

To continue to defend the homeland from Allied bombers, the Germans transferred all their fighters from the Russian front to the Western front. And despite introducing wonder weapons, like the ME262 jet aircraft, and the ME163 Komet rocket plane - whose impact was negligible, a case of too little, too late – the Luftwaffe seemed on the verge of collapse.

From lack of fuel, a shortage of pilots, and no safe airfields to operate from, the Luftwaffe often didn't respond to a bombing attack, and when it did, it responded with such small numbers of fighters that it was almost a suicide mission for the German pilots, with the odds sometimes 50 or 100-to-one against them.

As the US Eighth Air Force's new replacement pilots gained experience, the workload on the second-tour pilots was reduced. Matt and Jeff found they were often assigned to the 55th's A Group short-range tactical support missions, with one of them leading the flight and the other his wingman.

By early December, it seemed that the war was nearing an end, with the Eighth Air Force's strategic bombing campaign running out of targets to bomb.

A day or two of leave was now easier to get, and Jeff, remembering the promise he'd made to himself to make everything Matt had told his father in a letter about last year's Christmas Eve come true, was planning a surprise overnight trip back to Nuthampstead around Christmas Eve for him and Matt.

Then, on 16 December 1944, the weather, which was always bad that time of year in the UK for flying, worsened, and fog, combined with severe winter weather, grounded all Allied aircraft on the Western Front.

The Germans, who'd planned a counter-offensive based on bad weather eliminating the Allies' air superiority advantage and tactical air cover, attacked out of the Ardennes.

The battle that ensued, known as "The Battle of the Bulge," was one of the hardest-fought battles of the war for the Allied armies.

Allied pilots waited near their planes, at the ready should the weather improve enough to meet the bare minimum visibility for takeoff. But in the days when planes were rarely equipped with radar avoidance and with primitive air traffic control radar systems, the planes remained grounded.

Early on the morning of 24 December 1944, the weather improved just enough that Allied fighter and bomber commanders decided they would risk providing tactical support to their armies fighting but barely holding on in Belgium.

Eighth Air Force commanders were asked to select their most experienced pilots and to begin flying sorties to attack the German army fighting in Belgium.

At 0430, Matt and Jeff were awoken and ordered to report to the Briefing Room in 30 minutes.

Their mission was simple. Loose formations of P-51s - some armed with 1000-pound bombs, some with rockets - would proceed to their designated areas and attack anything that looked German, guided by spotters on the ground if possible.

When their ammo, fuel, or bombs were exhausted, they were to return to base, switch to another plane already armed and fueled, and return to their designated attack area.

Matt and Jeff each led a flight and made five sorties on the first day. They repeated the pattern the next day. As the weather cleared, more and more flights were added to the attack until the whole Group was engaged.

It wasn't until the middle of January 1945 that the number of daily sorties began to be reduced, and bomber-escort missions resumed. By then, all the Group's pilots were completely spent.

One night after the worst was over, when they were about to fall asleep, Jeff remembered the broken promise he'd made to himself to make Matt's imagined perfect Christmas Eve come true. He started to tell Matt about his intended plans and how sorry he was that he hadn't been able to make them happen.

Matt, who'd been in his own bed, got up and climbed into bed with Jeff, and hugging Jeff with all his might, trying to squeeze the sadness from him, said,

"You are amazing for even thinking of arranging something like that.

"I know about the postcards you've been sending my dad on the sly, telling him how I'm doing. You've already eased his mind a lot; he doesn't worry about me being lonely here anymore.

"And as far as me having a perfect Christmas Eve this year, I did: I got to spend it with you."

Then Matt gently kissed Jeff on the neck and cheek before going under the covers, heading for Jeff's feet and toes, saying, "I think the little guys are cold."

#

END OF SECOND TOUR-OF-DUTY: SEPARATION: MID-FEBRUARY 1945

On 22 February 1945, Colonel George T. Crowell's second tour of duty ended, and he handed command of the 55th Fighter Group to his successor, Lieutenant Colonel Elwyn G. Righetti. But an hour before he did, he signed a final order and then asked his adjutant to find First Lieutenants Yetman and Sullivan and tell them to report to him immediately.

When Matt and Jeff arrived, Colonel Crowell, wanting things to be kept formal, waited for them to snap-salute to report before saluting them and putting them at ease. With time short, he got right to the point.

"You probably know my tour is up today, and I'll shortly be handing my command over to Colonel Righetti. Before I did, I had one more order to sign.

"You each have over 400 hours flying combat, spent 16 months in a combat zone, flown well over 100 missions, and are on your second tour, so your tours of duty are ending today as well."

Matt started, "Permission to speak, sir," but the Colonel, knowing they'd both object, shook his head no and continued speaking.

"I'm using my personal prerogative as commander to order you two home. In my opinion, you're both suffering from combat fatigue.

"No arguments; the orders have already been cut. You leave on the next C-47 transport in one hour. Your line crew's tours are over, too, but they probably won't leave until next week."

The Colonel waited a moment before softly adding,

"We've tempted fate enough. You're leaving today with me," then thought to himself,

"I don't want to worry about these two being here in combat anymore. I only wish I could take all the second-tour pilots home with me today."

Then the Colonel shook their hands and said it had been an honor serving with them. Matt and Jeff tried to thank him for all he'd done, but he quickly dismissed them, saying, "You'd better hurry. You'll be in big trouble if you miss your flight."

Matt and Jeff picked up their orders from the adjutant, and judging they didn't have time to make it out to the flight line, asked that he let their line crews know what had happened and apologize to them for not having a chance to say goodbye.

They returned to the barracks and quickly packed their garment and small duffle bags and had just made it to the Air Transport Command hut when their names were called for boarding.

Their return flight followed the winter-ferrying route by way of the Azores, Bermuda, Florida, to New York. They slept through most legs of the flight, using each other as pillows.

When they landed at their last stop, Mitchell Field, Long Island, New York, at 0800 on Friday, 25 February 1945, new orders were waiting for them, separating them from active service, though they were still in the inactive reserves. They went to the base Quartermaster and collected their mustering-out pay before boarding a bus for Penn Station in New York City.

When they arrived at Penn Station, they each phoned home to let their families know they were safely in the States and would soon be home.

It wasn't until they were buying their tickets to different destinations - Jeff to Chicago, Matt to Boston - that it dawned on them what was happening: they were about to separate for the first time in ten months.

Their trains were leaving shortly on different platforms, so they shook hands to say goodbye. Jeff promised to phone as soon as he got home, then warned that it might not be until 10:00 am Matt's time.

They parted, and Jeff, whose train was about to leave with the final call already announced, disappeared into the crowd. Matt was about to turn and head for his train's boarding platform when Jeff, having dropped his bags, broke through the crowd and raced for Matt.

Not satisfied with a parting handshake, Jeff grabbed Matt and, in the middle of Penn Station, with them still wearing their uniforms, gave him a hug, saying,

"No worries. We'll meet soon. Promise me, no backsliding?" Matt returned the hug, then nodded yes to Jeff's question before Jeff released him and ran to catch his train.

Matt turned and walked away without looking back, unable to watch Jeff disappear again into the crowd. He wiped the tears from his eyes and thought, "Goodbye, Jeff."

CHAPTER 7 — HOME: MID-FEBRUARY TO MID-APRIL

1945

CATATONIC

Matt arrived home, exhausted, at around 6:30 pm. When his dad, Frank, opened the door, though, he had a rush of adrenaline and smiled, wrapping his arms around him, with the dog, Buster, going nuts, jumping all over him, trying to reach his face to lick him.

Matt and his dad held each other for a few moments in the doorway, before separating and entering the house. They settled in the living room and started to catch up while still trying to come to grips with all the quick changes.

Frank had noticed immediately Matt had changed physically, that he had filled out, no longer the boy he had seen off to war, leaving on the train to Boston more than two years earlier.

And he had noticed a change before in Matt's letters home after the middle of April of last year, a happiness that he hadn't sensed in Matt before. The same happiness Frank saw in the two pictures Captain Spiegel had given him when he visited last May, of Matt and his friend Jeff, now in full view on the reading table in front of them.

Frank knew that Matt had grown emotionally, come out of his shell and that that growth was all due to Jeff. And though Matt was obviously glad to be home, to be with him, he sensed that Matt was feeling a profound loss from being separated from Jeff. His suspicion was soon confirmed when he saw Matt wince when he noticed the pictures of them both in front of him.

Without trying to pry or draw Matt out about his feelings, in a matter-of-fact voice, Frank asked,

"So, where's Jeff? I was hoping you'd bring him home with you so I could finally get a chance to meet him."

Matt, who'd been avoiding discussing equally both the war and Jeff, replied,

"He's on the train to Chicago. He probably won't get home until ten or eleven tomorrow morning. He promised to call as soon as he got in, no matter what time it was.

"I'd have brought him home with me, but they sprang everything on us so quickly, we didn't have time to think.

"It all happened so fast. We didn't know we were being discharged until we landed at eight o'clock this morning. We thought we were going to be assigned as flight instructors somewhere down south or out west, maybe get a week's leave first."

Then, Matt wistfully added, "If we had it to do over again, maybe we'd do things differently, spend a few days around here before splitting up. But it's probably better this way; to make a clean break," Matt's voice cracking as he finished, betraying his emotion. He quickly bent over and hugged the dog, who hadn't left his side since he'd arrived, and tried to fight off the tears.

Frank, pretending not to notice, said,

"Well, when he calls, I want to speak to him, just to hear his voice. I guess you know he's been sending me a postcard every week, just a few words saying you were fine and promising to tell me if you weren't. That made all the difference to me. I want to thank him."

Matt, suddenly exhausted, feeling the effects of travel, the time-zone changes, and his emotions, apologized and said he needed to lie down for a while.

Frank said no worries and that he'd wake Matt when Jeff called if he was still asleep. But then added he thought Matt should try to eat something first. He'd just made a pot of clam chowder and tempted Matt with a bowl.

Matt, wanting to please his dad but also suddenly remembering how much he loved his dad's clam chowder, sat with his dad at the kitchen table and had a bowl, before climbing the stairs to his room for a nap, with Buster leading the way.

As soon as his train, Pennsylvania Railroad's No. 75, had pulled from the station, less than five minutes into the 21-and-a-half-hour trip, Jeff knew he'd made a mistake leaving Matt without them having made firm plans for getting back together.

He could have stayed with Matt in Massachusetts for a few days to meet his dad, then taken Matt with him back to Illinois to meet his family. That would have given them plenty of time to plan what to do next. But now he was stuck on an express train to Chicago that only made a few short stops, so he had no way of getting a message to Matt.

He spent the trip alternately kicking himself for being so foolish and thinking about how much Matt meant to him. Although Matt had promised no backsliding, Jeff, knowing Matt better than anyone, worried he was doing just that.

When Jeff arrived at Chicago's Union Station at 7:40 am central time the next morning, he found his mom and dad waiting for him on the platform.

He hugged and kissed them both, including his dad - something he now felt comfortable doing after being with Matt - and together, they made their way to his parent's car, a 1940 Folkstone grey Ford Super Deluxe "Woody" station wagon, the car Jeff learned to drive on and loved to borrow when he was in high school.

Jeff got in the front seat between his mom and dad.

For the half hour-ride home to Oak Park, in the Irish neighborhood of the family-friendly suburb of Chicago where Jeff grew up, his dad asked Jeff questions, about his health, service status, and then eventually zeroed in on Matt, where he was, how he was doing.

Jeff answered all his dad's questions as best he could and basked in the love of his parents, with his mom sitting beside him to his right, satisfied with just holding his hand.

When they arrived home, there was a large group of family members waiting for them, and Jeff was mauled by another round of hugs and kisses. The result was it took another hour before Jeff could break away to his parent's room for some privacy to phone Matt.

Matt, whose body clock hadn't reset yet from Greenwich Mean Time (GMT), had gotten up early, before his dad, around 5:30 am. Since it was a Saturday, his dad would be home all day, and Matt thought he'd probably sleep for another hour or two. So, Matt took Buster for a walk along the beach.

The sun was just rising, and they had the beach to themselves. As a kid, and especially when he was in high school, he and Buster would always walk this stretch of shore whenever he had some problem to work out. The quiet and open view seaward always had a calming effect on him, and this time was no different. By the time they got back, about an hour later, Matt felt better about his decision to let Jeff go now that the war was over, to not hold him back from a normal life. He loved Jeff so much;

somehow, he'd find the strength to do the right thing and let him go.

Despite what Matt thought, Frank was up when he heard Matt leave for his walk. In fact, he'd been up all night worrying about Matt. When he heard Matt return, he got up and dressed, then went downstairs to the kitchen.

He found Matt sitting at the kitchen table, staring into space, patting Buster. Matt greeted his dad with a cheery "Morning, Dad," then got up and gave him a hug.

When Matt hugged him, Frank sensed a deep sadness in him. Frank knew Matt was hurting, putting on a brave face for him. But he didn't confront the problem head-on: he knew that wouldn't work. He had a good idea of what Matt was thinking and had spent the night devising a plan of his own. It all depended on if he had an ally in Jeff. From all he knew about Jeff, he was sure he did. Today's phone call from him would confirm that.

Without asking if he was hungry, Frank made Matt and himself a big breakfast. He steered the conversation away from the war, or Jeff, and tried to distract Matt by talking about his work at General Electric in nearby Lynn, Massachusetts: Frank, an MIT graduate, had worked there as a mechanical engineer for 15 years, mostly on the turbochargers used on P-38 and P-47 fighters, and B-17 and B-24 bombers, but had recently become involved in developing GE's new jet engine design, based on turbocharger high-temperature materials and precision-machining technologies. Most of the work was classified, but at that moment, Frank didn't care.

Frank noticed while they were eating that Matt only picked at his food and that any food that disappeared from his plate had been fed to Buster. He also noticed Matt hadn't showered.

He and Jeff had spent three days flying back from England, with only brief stops to refuel at the ferrying-route airfields. And he'd been on a train all day the day before. So, it had probably been at least a week since Matt had showered or shaved properly. He was starting to look a little scruffy and to smell a little, but he didn't seem to notice or care.

Frank knew that not eating or grooming properly were two signs that Matt was experiencing depression. Matt had been depressed before, in high school, when he'd severed his friendship with his best friend, Peter Kingman, for some reason but only stopped eating and sleeping; he'd never let himself go physically. Frank thought this time, Matt's depression must be much worse. But again, he pretended not to notice.

They spent the morning quietly together, with Frank deliberately touching Matt as often as possible, putting an arm around his shoulder or briefly rubbing his back, waiting for Jeff's call.

As it came closer to the expected time for Jeff to call, Frank noticed Matt becoming tenser, seemingly filled with dread, while Frank was anxiously waiting now, with a growing sense of urgency.

At 10:40 am, a little later than expected, the phone rang. Frank waited for Matt to pick it up to answer, but when he didn't move after three rings, Frank picked up the phone.

Frank said, "Hello, Jeff. It's Frank Yetman."

Jeff said, "Hello, Mr. Yetman. It's great to finally hear your voice."

Frank said, "It's great to finally hear yours, too. And please call me Frank. Before I hand you over to Matt, can I have your phone number? I'm sure Matt has it, but I just want to be sure I can reach you."

Jeff instantly read between the lines, gave Frank his number, and thanked him for the subtle message. Then Frank handed the phone to Matt.

Matt, summoning all his emotional strength, said, "Hi, Jeff. Did you make it home OK? Are you all right?"

Jeff answered, "I'm fine, Matt. I'm sorry for calling a little late: there must be a hundred people here, and I had trouble getting away. Are you OK?"

Matt answered he was and, looking at his dad, said, "It's been good seeing my dad again. I missed him so much."

Running out of time on the three-and-a-half-minute long-distance call, Jeff said,

"I messed up. I should have gone home with you for a few days to meet your dad, then dragged you out here to meet my family. I'm getting a lot of flak from them for not bringing you home with me.

"You have to bail me out. You have to come out here right away; take the next train. I'm toast if you don't."

Matt said, "I can't come out right now. I just got back home, and I don't want to leave my dad so soon."

Jeff, really worried now, asked,

"Well, when can you come? How about early next week? No worries, I'll meet you at the train station in Chicago, and I promise it'll just be me picking you up."

When Matt didn't say yes, Jeff, desperate now, said, "We'll have plenty of time to talk, to plan things. We need a chance to talk."

Matt, now crying, but trying to hide it from Jeff, said,

"Ah, next week, I'm supposed to try to enroll back at MIT for the fall. Maybe in a few weeks. I can write and let you know for sure."

Just then, the long-distance operator interrupted, saying, "Your three-and-a-half minutes are nearly up, sir. Would you like to extend the call?"

Jeff yelled, "Yes," but Matt quickly ended the call, saying,

"No. This is costing you a fortune, and your family is waiting. I promise I'll call you, maybe tomorrow. Thanks for calling, Jeff, and letting me know you're safe."

Jeff just managed to get out, "I love you, Matt," before he heard Matt hang up.

Matt, with his arms crossed and resting on top of his head, and his head tilted back, staring at the ceiling, had forgotten his dad was in the room, and was openly weeping.

Frank, who had only heard Matt's side of the conversation, but had guessed what Jeff had said, just went to Matt, who was still standing by the phone, and pulled him into an embrace, and without saying a word, held him and let him cry it out.

After about 15 minutes, Matt stopped crying and said,

"Thanks, Dad. It's better this way for him. He deserves a normal life."

Frank said, as gently as he could,

"I know you love him; enough to give him up.

"But you're not being fair to him. You've made up your mind about what's best for him without asking him what he wants.

"And I think you're wrong about what's best for him. You're what's best for him, and he knows it. And he's what's best for you, and I know it.

"You've been wrong about him before, more than once - Captain Spiegel told me when he visited to give me your pictures, we had a good chat. Jeff had to almost drown himself to prove to you he loved you.

"You're wrong about him now if you think he's going to let you go without a fight. If you want him to go, you're going to have to tell him you don't love him to his face, not over the phone, when he's 850 miles away and can't hold you to know if you're being honest with him."

Matt, exhausted, was crying again. His dad had never spoken to him like that before. He knew his dad meant well and was shocked that he was fully aware of the depth of Matt and Jeff's friendship and didn't care; he was even supportive.

But he thought his dad didn't understand. It was OK for Matt to be close to Jeff while they were in combat and could help each other survive. Now that they were out of the service, that closeness could cost Jeff the respect of his family and friends, and deny him a chance to have a family of his own, something Matt really wanted for him.

Too tired to process anything anymore, Matt hugged his dad and thanked him for being there for him before going up to his room to sleep.

Matt had barely shut his bedroom door before Frank was on the phone, dialing the long-distance operator.

#

SWAMPSCOTT

Matt stayed in his room for the rest of the day and night, refusing offers of food from his dad, saying he was catching up on his sleep. But Frank knew better; he could hear Matt sobbing through the door.

When Matt finally reappeared, around 10:00 am the next day, Sunday, he looked much worse than he had the day before. It was obvious he hadn't slept that night, and probably not in days, and he turned down his dad's offer to cook him breakfast, saying he was going to take Buster for another walk on the beach.

When he came back an hour later, Frank tried to get Matt to at least drink some water, which Matt did, but more to please his dad than from any thirst. Then he went back to his room.

Late in the afternoon, around 5:30 pm, Frank climbed the stairs and knocked on Matt's door. He asked Matt to come downstairs; he needed his help with something in the living room.

When Matt arrived, he found Jeff standing there.

Jeff, crying a little as he wrapped his arms around Matt, tenderly said,

"You promised no backsliding."

Matt, almost comatose now, wasn't sure if he was dreaming or not.

Frank, also crying, said, "Jeff, why don't you take Matt up to his - I mean yours and Matt's room - for a little nap."

Jeff said, "Yes, that's a good idea. But we stink a little and need to take a shower first.

"When we're done, maybe we could grab a sandwich or something? We're both hungry and thirsty. We only need one plate and glass; we can share."

Matt, totally compliant now, let Jeff lead him upstairs. Jeff quickly found Matt's room and led Matt in. He opened the dresser and found two clean pairs of underwear for them: Jeff had left home without packing, rushing to make the first train to Boston.

Matt was just standing in the middle of the room. Jeff quickly undressed himself, then undressed Matt. Then, naked and carrying their clean underwear, he led Matt to the bathroom.

Jeff started the shower, then helped Matt in before climbing in himself. He quickly washed himself, then started on Matt.

Under the spray of the hot water, Matt, who still hadn't spoken, began to revive and grunt a little, which Jeff took as a good sign. Jeff kept up a banter of small talk, saying how good Matt was doing when asked to raise or lower his arms or turn for him.

Matt was pretty dirty, like a usually fastidious cat that had gotten sick and let himself go. His hair was tangled, and his butt was dirty, so it took Jeff a while to get him clean.

When they finished their shower, Jeff dried them, then brought them to the sink. He opened the medicine cabinet and found a razor. Not caring whose it was, he lathered Matt's face, then gently shaved him before shaving himself.

Then he looked for a toothbrush. He found two in a glass and selected one, then asked Matt if it was his. When Matt didn't answer, Jeff, figuring he had a fifty-fifty chance that it was Matt's, brushed Matt's teeth and then his own.

He combed their hair, then put their boxers on, and smiling, happy with his handiwork, said, "There you go, you're beautiful again," before taking them back to Matt's room to find a couple of t-shirts. Then, in just their underwear, Jeff led them down to the kitchen.

Frank had done what Jeff asked and set a single place for the two of them and one for himself. He'd warmed the clam chowder, had made them ham and cheese sandwiches, and poured them a glass of milk.

Jeff scooted two chairs together at their place setting, maneuvered Matt into a chair, and then sat beside him, making sure their bare legs touched.

Jeff said to Frank, "Thanks, Frank. This looks great. We're starving."

Jeff took a bite of a sandwich, then offered Matt a bite. When he didn't respond, Jeff said,

"I'm not eating if you don't," offering a bite of the sandwich again.

When this time Matt took a bite, Frank, despite himself, let out a groan in relief.

Jeff, pretending not to notice anything, just kept up his encouraging banter with Matt, now while also rubbing Matt's back.

He handed the sandwich to Matt, saying, "Here, we'll share. You first. I want to keep rubbing your back; you've got goosebumps and feel a little cold," then dragged the mug of hot chowder over and said, "You need to eat some of this, too. It'll warm you up."

Frank noticed that Jeff wasn't being pushy or forceful with Matt. It was just that Matt trusted Jeff so much; he followed his directions unquestioningly. He also noticed that, although they were supposed to be sharing, Jeff often pretended to lose track of whose turn it was, then always decided it was Matt's turn, getting him to eat more.

When they'd finished dinner, Jeff thanked Frank again, and said they were tired and going to bed, then warned him not to worry if he heard a lot of loud snoring.

As they were leaving the kitchen and Buster stirred to go with them, Jeff asked Frank if he'd mind keeping Buster in his room for the night: Matt's bed was kind of small for the three of them, and he thought they'd get a better sleep the first night if it was just the two of them. Frank smiled and, looking at Buster, said,

"Hey, boy. Looks like you're bunking with me tonight. No worries, Matt's in very good hands."

Jeff led Matt back to their room, turned down the bed, and helped Matt in before climbing in after him. He wrapped an arm around Matt, pulled him in tight, and softly said,

"Have a good sleep, Matt; you need it. I'll be right here when you wake up. I'm not going anywhere; you're stuck with me." Then added, " I love you so much," and kissed him on the nap of the neck.

When Jeff awoke the next morning and opened his eyes, he found Matt staring back at him. Matt kissed him and then said,

"Thank you for coming back. I'm sorry you had to leave your family. You were probably only home for 15 minutes."

Jeff, smiling, said, "No worries. I was home for at least an hour; they were probably getting sick of me already.

"The person we should thank is your dad. I was a wreck after you hung up; my parents found me and couldn't do anything with me.

"Then your dad called back 15 minutes later. My dad answered the phone and didn't realize it was your dad, so he tried to put him off and said I'd call him back later. Whatever your dad said was pretty forceful because my dad handed me the phone in a hurry, then took my mom and left the room.

"When I heard your dad on the phone, I lost it. He waited a few minutes, waving the long-distance operator off, until I got myself under control. Then he asked me a few direct questions to satisfy himself I wanted to be with you. Only then did he describe your condition.

"He also told me how you got so bad: of your plan of a clean break from me so I could have a normal life. Then he asked me point-blank, did I want that?

"When I told him absolutely not, he told me you didn't either, that you loved me, and if you said otherwise, to dare you to tell me to my face while I was holding you, and that you wouldn't be able to do it.

"Then, your dad took charge of the situation. He said he was sorry, but I had to leave for Boston right away. Not to wait to pack but to ask my parents to take me back to the station. There'd be a ticket waiting for me. He gave me directions for how to get from South Station in Boston to North Station to catch the train to Swampscott and how to find your house. He said to call if I had any issues along the way; he'd figure a way around any problems, even if it meant me taking a cab all the way from Illinois. I think he meant it.

"Then he asked to speak with my dad. They were only on the phone for a minute, and I saw my dad switch to emergency mode, and now it was his mission to get me to the train on time. My mom, who loves you already and has never even met you yet, rushed us out of the house, saying to my relatives something important had come up, and I had to go to Boston to save a friend.

"When I got to the station, there was a ticket waiting for me – for a room in a sleeping car! I don't know how your dad did it.

"I kissed my parents goodbye and said I'd be back soon with you. Both my mom and dad said I'd be in big trouble if I didn't.

"Everything went like clockwork. I don't know what your dad does for a living, but he's a logistics genius.

"I had time to think on the train. There was another hand at work here. Your dad's directness, his accurate reading of us, it all felt very familiar. I think he was tutored by the master, Captain Spiegel."

Matt said, "Yes, he spoke to me Saturday after our call, directly, like he never had before. He did say Captain Spiegel and him had a chat when he visited to bring him our pictures.

"Sounds like my dad knew what to do, almost like he expected this to happen and was prepared."

"And my parents didn't protest my leaving at all, as if they had at least some idea there could be a problem, especially if I didn't come home with you. Your dad and mine might have been given a code word to use between them to trigger an emergency response. Your dad wasn't on the phone with mine two seconds before I was rushed out the door. It felt like I was in labor, having a baby."

They both agreed; the mystery was solved. Captain Spiegel had anticipated Matt's backsliding and had built a firewall with both their parents just in case. He'd probably devised the contingency plan when he borrowed the camera used to take their pictures at the pool a year before.

For the first time in days, Frank slept well, so well he didn't wake until his alarm clock went off at 6:30 am. When he shut the alarm off, he could hear voices coming from the kitchen and noticed Buster was gone: he'd left the door open for him. He got up and put his robe on, then went downstairs.

He found Matt and Jeff, wearing t-shirts and jeans and in their bare feet, goofing off making breakfast but keeping their voices down in case Frank was trying to get a few more minutes of sleep.

When they saw him, they formed a line with Matt first.

Matt said, "Morning, Dad. Thank you for everything," giving him a big hug, closely followed by Jeff, who said, "Morning, Frank. We hope you're hungry; we've made you breakfast," giving him just as big a hug.

Frank, looking at the spread before him of pancakes, toast, bacon and eggs, and pan-fried potatoes, said,

"This looks great. How long have you two been up? This took a while."

Matt, smiling, with his arm around Jeff, said,

"We've only been up a little while.

"Jeff's a great cook; he did all the work. You know I'm a lousy cook; I can burn water. I just made the toast and stirred the batter.

Jeff said, "No way, you're much better than that. And you made the coffee."

They had a great breakfast. Frank asked what their plans were for the day, and Matt said he thought they'd walk the beach and he'd show Jeff some of Swampscott.

Frank offered the car, saying he didn't need it; he'd take the train to work: there was a stop right in front of GE. But then he planted another seed of his plan.

Following Captain Spiegel's advice to always be direct, he started.

"Have you guys thought about re-enrolling in college?"

Matt and Jeff said they had, and were thinking about starting again in the fall, Matt at MIT in Cambridge and Jeff at Illinois Institute of Technologies in Chicago.

Frank said, " You know about the G.I. Bill, right?"

Matt and Jeff had heard something about it but weren't too sure what it was all about.

Frank said, "Well, Roosevelt signed it last July, and it basically provides tuition and living assistance to any serviceman returning from the war. It will basically cover the cost of your tuition and books and give you a little extra for food and housing. You're both eligible.

"It's a hell of a deal, a sort of thank you for serving from the country. I expect there will be a stampede once the first wave of servicemen gets discharged.

"You're very lucky to have been let out early, ahead of the rush. The colleges are half full right now. If you hurry, I'm sure you can get signed up for benefits and registered for the fall."

Frank let Matt and Jeff absorb the news: they had both finished their sophomore year -satisfying the USAAF's requirement of two years of technical school to become a pilot – when they'd enlisted. And they were both majoring in aeronautical engineering. Then he made his pitch.

"Why do you have to go to separate schools?

"You're both aero-majors, ready to start your junior year. You've both been away from the books and math for a couple of years, and you'll be competing against some pretty smart guys with everything fresh in their minds.

"You'd be taking the same classes together and could help each other out, even things up. Plus, you have all the practical knowledge the guys that didn't serve won't have. Especially being pilots, taking aeronautical engineering, you'd have a huge advantage."

Then, looking at Matt, said,

"Of course, you'd be spending a lot of time studying and living together. Maybe it'd be too much, and you'd get tired of each other."

That worked; Matt was on board. But then he dashed Frank's hopes by saying,

"Jeff, I'd be willing to transfer. Do you think your parents would let me room with you?"

But Jeff, who looked at Frank's crest-fallen expression, had caught on and said,

"I think it would be better if I transferred here. Doolittle got his Ph.D. in aero from MIT: the first one awarded in the US. And they have a new wind tunnel, the Wright Brothers Wind Tunnel. Maybe we could work there part-time; that would be great experience. That's how Kelly Johnson got started.

"Frank, could I live here for a while? From what you're saying, I could afford to pay rent."

Matt looked pleadingly at Frank, but only for an instant before Frank said,

"I'd love to have you stay here. No worries about room and board; you and Matt could use any extra money to take the pressure off and enjoy your time in college. Maybe Matt could show you how to ski next winter; he's pretty good at it, you know."

Jeff didn't know Matt could ski but should have guessed by now, wondering again if there was anything this guy couldn't do.

Frank got up to get ready for work and asked them to think about it, then not-so-subtly reminded Matt that MIT's admission office was open, they could take the train to North Station and walk to campus, or take the subway. Then kissed them both on the top of the head before climbing the stairs to his room. Once he'd shut his bedroom door, he dropped his mask of impartial adviser and wept from relief. He thought, thank God for Captain Spiegel; he'd been right about everything.

#

LUCK OF THE IRISH

Thomas Willard © 2021

Matt and Jeff went to MIT that day and signed the forms to apply for G.I. Bill benefits. Matt also applied to enroll in the fall, and Jeff applied to transfer and enroll. They were assured there would be no problems and that they would receive confirmation of their benefits eligibility and fall enrollment by mail in early June.

That evening, during supper, they let Frank know they'd completed the paperwork to enroll for the fall semester. Frank said great but then offered another idea.

It wasn't fair that he'd taken Jeff away from his family after just getting home. Maybe they should go to Chicago and visit for a month or so, especially now that Jeff was going to transfer to MIT and be away from home for a couple of years, though he thought Jeff should promise his folks he'd make it back home at least for the holidays and spring break.

Matt and Jeff thought that was a great idea. Jeff was immediately enthused about showing Matt around Chicago, and if they hurried, they'd make the Saint Patrick's Day parade: Jeff being Irish, knew all the good spots, and his dad loved the celebration. Jeff was also keen to introduce Matt to his parents, especially his mom, who, knowing Matt's mother had died when he was still a toddler, was looking forward to not replacing Matt's mom but mothering him to pieces anyway, though Jeff thought it best not to warn Matt of her intentions.

Frank then offered to splurge on sleeper tickets if they wanted to go by train, or they could go on a road trip: they could use his car; he didn't need it.

They decided to go by car - that way, they could bring Jeff's books and clothes back with them. And to make it in time for Saint Patrick's Day, they decided to leave early the next day before Frank was up.

So, after cleaning up from supper and taking Buster out for a walk on the beach, they packed a few things in Matt's B-4 bag, took a shower together, then hugged and kissed Frank goodnight - saying goodbye, but they'd be back soon - before going to bed.

They were up and on the road by 4:00 am. For the two former-fighter pilots, the approximately 940-mile trip along US20 was a breeze. They drove straight through in a little over 17 hours, changing drivers every three or four hours to let the other sleep, using the driver's legs as a pillow.

When they pulled into Jeff's driveway the next day at around 7:00 pm, they were warmly greeted with hugs from both his parents. Then, after kissing her son, Jeff's mother, Rose, kissed Matt and then, as Jeff expected, immediately started mothering him.

Matt, surprising Jeff, took all the attention and affection in stride. To Matt, it was Jeff's mom and dad, and anything Jeff was good with him, even letting his mom hold his hand.

Jeff's dad, Michael, made a few phone calls, and soon, the house was full of relatives. It seemed to Matt that Jeff had a million aunts, uncles, cousins, nieces, and nephews, all living in the same neighborhood, many with similar facial features as Jeff, so Matt felt strangely comfortable. Jeff's brothers were all in the service, so Matt would have to wait to meet them on another visit.

All the family obviously adored Jeff and were not shy about expressing it: there was none of the New England reserve that Matt was used to, and Matt loved seeing all that affection being showered on Jeff.

It seemed like there was always someone trying to pull Jeff aside, to show him something, or to bring him somewhere to speak more privately with a relative or group, or in the case of the little kids, to play with him. Jeff would smile, let his younger nieces and nephews climb all over him, and pull him, but he wouldn't budge from Matt's side.

Magically from somewhere, plates of corn beef and cabbage with boiled potatoes - Jeff's favorite - appeared, with Irish soda bread and butter.

Whether they had been warned in advance to be gentle with Matt or not, everyone was friendly with Matt, but no one pushed themselves on him, crowded him, or was too familiar with him in any way. The adults mostly just came by to shake his hand and say they were very glad to meet him. And no one seemed to stare at him but reserved their attention for Jeff.

Rose would come by every now and then and hold his hand before she had to return to the kitchen to help with the food, but she seemed like the only one with permission to touch him, other than Jeff.

Finally, around 9:00 pm, when it was well past the bedtime of all the little guys, the informal party started to break up. As everyone left, they'd stop to hug Jeff again, then wave goodbye to Matt. Some brave souls even risked Rose's wrath and patted Matt on the shoulders.

When Matt and Jeff appeared in the kitchen to help with the clean-up, they were promptly escorted out by several of Jeff's aunts and older female cousins and told to say goodnight to Jeff's mom and dad and to go to bed.

They hunted Jeff's mom and dad down and said they'd been ordered to bed by the kitchen crew, who were not to be disobeyed. Jeff's dad hugged them both, saying how happy he was they were there, then his mom hugged and kissed them both before sending them upstairs, telling them they looked tired, not to worry about sleeping late, and for Matt to pick any of Jeff's brothers' beds, they all had clean sheets.

Grabbing their B-4 bag, Jeff led Matt up to his room. The room was just as Jeff had described it, with five beds closely spaced against the walls. Jeff's bed was the last to the right as you entered the room. The room felt masculine to Matt but warm and comfortable, and he thought how the room matched Jeff perfectly.

Jeff closed the door and locked it, then threw the B-4 bag on the bed next to his. They hugged each other and started to undress but remembered they needed to visit the bathroom and brush their teeth first. They walked to the bathroom together, but when Jeff went in, Matt waited outside. When Jeff finished, Matt went in but closed the door.

Jeff went back to his room and waited for Matt, wondering what was happening. When Matt returned, Jeff locked the door behind him and pulled him in for a hug. Matt hugged him back with all his might and kissed him, so Jeff thought everything was back to normal. They got undressed, down to their underwear, and Jeff turned his bed down. But Matt had taken the B-4 bag and placed it on the floor and turned down that bed, too.

Confused, Jeff climbed into his bed and pulled up the covers, and waited for Matt to do the same thing in his bed. Then he asked,

"Matt. Is there anything wrong? Have I upset you somehow?"

Matt took a while to answer, to think how to explain himself, then said,

"You're Irish Catholic, right? Your whole family?

"They all love you so much. I can't let you do anything that would risk your losing their respect for you.

"I love you, and I always will. But what would your family think, your parents and brothers think, if they knew we were romantically involved?

"I think they can turn a blind eye if we are affectionate with each other, even allow that we love each other, are as close as twins. But they could never accept or understand if we go past a certain point.

"I'd feel really disrespectful to your mother and father if I violated their trust while in their home. But much, much worse if I did anything to diminish you in their eyes."

Jeff didn't have an easy answer for Matt. He knew his mom and dad would love Matt once they'd met him. And they more than supported his going to Boston to help and get him, probably due to some prepping from Captain Spiegel. But unlike Matt's dad, he wasn't sure how explicit Captain Spiegel had been with his family.

He knew Captain Spiegel would never divulge any private information unless he knew it was safe and that he'd created a pretext to visit and interview their families. It seems Captain Spiegel had chosen to be more explicit with Matt's dad than with his mom and dad, providing them with just enough information to get their support to help save Matt from backsliding. So, Jeff, now even more glad that he'd decided to transfer instead of Matt, said,

"Matt, I respect your decision. You're an honorable person; that's one of the reasons I love you so much.

"While we're here, we'll do nothing, in public or private, that we wouldn't want everyone else to see. But I'm warning you, when it comes to public displays of affection, I'm going to push your limits. I want my family to see how much I love you. I expect you to return the affection, not just accept it.

"But we're going to talk when we get back. You can't decide for the both of us anymore on things like this, or I'll tell your dad on you, and you won't like it when he comes down hard. He's my best ally, and I'm going to use him, even if it's unfair, two against one. Is it a deal?"

Matt said it was a deal. Then Jeff asked, "Are backrubs in private out-of-bounds?"

Matt said he wasn't sure but thought maybe they were. So, Jeff said,

"Ok, fine. I don't mind you giving me a backrub in front of my family, so that will be the first test."

That changed Matt's mind fast, and he agreed to give Jeff a back rub, justifying it to himself because he knew that in the back of his mind, he wasn't trying to get Jeff to do anything more and wouldn't care if his mom and dad saw them. Of course, Jeff knew he really did care: that's why he'd changed his mind.

While Matt was giving Jeff a back rub, Jeff thought about Matt's decision. It might have been the right thing to do after all.

Matt was too honest and knew he couldn't hide looking guilty for doing anything Jeff's parents wouldn't approve of. So, by their remaining celibate during their stay, there'd be nothing to feel guilty about. Jeff, much better at the art of deceiving his parents, having been taught by four masters of the art, could sympathize with Matt's dilemma.

So, Jeff let Matt off the hook.

"Matt, I'm sorry. I don't want you to feel uncomfortable while you're here. I won't push you into doing anything too publicly affectionate. I would like my parents to know that I love you, but I want them to see that it's mutual.

"You can tell my family is very affectionate; anything they do is in-bounds. But even that might be too much for you; it takes some getting used to.

"I'll take my cues from you. Push yourself a little, but I'll limit myself to what you do to me. OK?"

Matt was feeling relief from Jeff's rescinding his deal but was also very horny from giving Jeff a back rub. He hoped Jeff didn't notice.

In a slightly pitched voice, Matt, twisting away from Jeff, trying to hide his arousal, said, "Ah, OK. That sounds good."

Jeff, knowing exactly what Matt was up to, smiled and said, "Great, that's settled," then added, "Try not to moan too much when you take care of that; I'm horny enough as it is. Oh, and be careful: my mom checks the sheets."

#

ON THE MOORING

In the middle of April, Matt and Jeff returned to Swampscott. Unlike on the ride out, when they'd driven straight through, they took their time on the ride back and stopped for a few days in the Berkshires in Massachusetts to explore the area.

Jeff had fully expected their celibacy to end the moment they pulled out of his parent's driveway, but he was frustrated to learn that Matt, more than ever, was determined to keep their relationship platonic. It seems his mom, by plan or not, and obviously worried about their womanizing, had made Matt promise not to lead Jeff astray, and Matt had expanded that to include himself.

Jeff, totally aware of the power of Irish guilt, especially coming from his mom, was now completely frustrated and at a loss as to what to do.

Thomas Willard © 2021

They left Lenox, Massachusetts, for the final leg of the drive home around 5:00 am on a Saturday morning and pulled into Matt's driveway at around 8:00 am.

Frank was there to welcome them, hugging them together, then kissing their foreheads before releasing them.

As soon as he had a chance, when Matt had gone to the bathroom, Jeff cornered Frank and explained his problem.

Unhelpfully, at first, Frank just laughed. But when he saw how desperate Jeff was, he stopped his teasing and told Jeff he thought he knew a way to help. So, he explained his idea.

"I'm sorry for laughing. And bear with me if I beat around the bush a little: if I'm too circumspect. We're still haunted by the ghosts of the Puritans around here.

"There are some things about Matt you might not fully appreciate yet.

"I don't think you realize it because you've put Matt up on such a high pedestal, but he cares for you more than you can imagine. I mean, he really cares. A lot. In a good way. Are you getting my drift?

"I've seen the way he looks at you. There is a lot of his mother in him, and I remember that look. If it means what I think it does, you could be in big trouble. I mean, in a good way. Just drink a lot of water, and keep yourself hydrated.

"The other thing is, just like his mother, Matt is a hopeless romantic. He loves the ocean. And especially sailing. Nothing brought out the romantic in his mother like sailing. The wind, the water, sailing, the beautiful scenery, and you. It all will have an effect on him, in a good way.

"Matt hasn't been sailing for a while. And from what you just told me, he hasn't done something else in a while.

"So, here's my recipe for success. A sailboat, Marblehead harbor at sunset, and you. A beer or two couldn't hurt."

Just then, Matt bounded down the stairs and said,

"Hey, what are you guys talking about?"

Frank said, "We were just discussing the roots of success, and I'm really rooting for Jeff," then he said he needed to make a phone call and he'd be back in a minute.

Jeff went up to use the bathroom, and when he got back, Frank was just returning from making his call. Frank said,

"I called the boat yard, and they can launch the boat today.

"Matt, let me drop you two off in Marblehead, and you can give Jeff a tour while you're waiting for the boat. Check out Abbot Hall and the Spirit of '76, and take him to The Landing for fried clams.

"I know the owner of Willard's Mooring Service, and he'll let you stay on a mooring tonight. Then you can sail back tomorrow. How's that?"

Matt was beside himself. He hugged his dad, then said to Jeff,

"This is so great. You'll love it, I promise. The boat is so beautiful. Oh, man!"

Frank looked at Jeff and smiled, then said, giving him a thumbs up, "To success. And I wouldn't worry about the beer."

But then Matt, all enthused, said, "Dad, why don't you come with us? It'll be great!" getting a quick, simultaneous "NO!" from Frank and Jeff.

Frank dropped them off in the Old Town section of Marblehead, and they spent the afternoon visiting Abbot Hall and exploring the colonial-era neighborhood before making their way down to the waterfront. They ate an early supper of fried clams at The Landing watching the Marblehead Trading Company crew finish stepping and rigging the mast.

Around 5:30 pm, they got the signal that the boat was ready, and they walked down the long ramp to the floating dock next to the fuel dock where the boat was tied up.

Matt filled the boat with fuel and, paid the attendant, then started the engine. He asked Jeff to man the helm while he cast off all the lines, then quickly took the helm and backed the boat from the dock.

As they motored to their mooring in front of the Corinthian Yacht Club, Matt explained to Jeff how to catch the mooring pennant with the boat hook. They managed to hook the pennant on the first try, and Jeff attached it to the bow cleat before Matt turned off the engine.

The sun was just setting, and there was a bit of a chill in the air, but it was a beautiful evening. It was very early in the season, and they practically had the harbor to themselves.

Their bow was pointing at Marblehead Light off the north point of Marblehead Neck, towards the open sea, and there was a gentle five-knot sea breeze blowing.

Jeff, who'd never been on a small boat on the ocean before, was mesmerized. And he couldn't believe how natural Matt was on the boat.

He'd first thought Matt was in his element in the air, then he thought it was in a pool, but now he knew it was when he was on a sailboat. And they hadn't even sailed yet. What was he going to be like tomorrow, sailing to Swampscott? He couldn't wait to find out and for Matt to teach him everything he knew about sailing.

Matt, though, was thinking about something else. About how beautiful the boat looked in the twilight, about how beautiful Marblehead harbor looked, and how beautiful Jeff looked on the boat in Marblehead Harbor at twilight.

Jeff first noticed Matt was near him when he placed his hands on his shoulders. Then Jeff felt Matt's body getting closer, then a lot closer, pressing into him. He felt a particular part of Matt really pressing against him, then turned so they were face-to-face, so his particular body part could press into Matt's.

Matt kissed Jeff with more passion than Jeff thought Matt was capable of. Then Matt started undressing Jeff, outdoors, on deck. Jeff liked the idea of being naked outdoors but wasn't going to be the only one, so he started stripping Matt.

When they were both down to just their underwear, they pushed themselves together and then kissed while pulling each other's boxers down and then off.

They both gasped when their bare manhoods touched. The soft breeze on their naked bodies felt like a million hands were gently caressing them. The erotic feeling of being naked, outdoors, in the arms of the person they loved, kissing, with their hard, leaking penises pressed together, in one of the most beautiful places on earth, proved too much, and they came, hard, together, soaking each other.

They sat in the cockpit, so recently living up to its name, and basked in the afterglow, holding each other for warmth and comfort. Matt, usually the shy one, felt primal, finally fully able to express his love for Jeff.

After a few minutes, Jeff spoke.

"I don't agree with what you said about us in Chicago: that we're somehow disgusting, a disgrace, and our families, really mine, would disown me if they found out we were romantically involved. And that you're a corrupting influence on me.

"You may be right about how my family – not all, but maybe some – would react. Captain Spiegel might have thought that, too, so he kept the most important private details about us from them.

"But I don't think we're disgusting, and I especially don't think you are. You're the finest person I know or I am ever going to know. I love you, and I'm proud of it. I'm amazed you'd want anything to do with me, let alone love me. I still get goosebumps every time you touch me, and I can't believe it when I get to touch you.

"You're beautiful; what we do together is beautiful: I feel like we're in ancient Greece sometimes. I'm not ashamed of any of it. If we have to keep our sexual acts private, well, who doesn't? Except for Mrs. Frobisher, no one wants a show.

"I think Captain Spiegel was right: with our history, our family and friends expect us to be close; we don't have to hide our love and affection from them. They'll give us a pass, be blind to anything else, as long as we don't confront them with it.

"I'll probably tell my brothers at some point, at least the ones I think can deal with it, starting with my youngest brother, Patrick.

"And, for the record, I corrupted you, remember? I don't think you could even spell sex until you met me. I did it, and I'm glad, though; it's the best thing I've ever done.

"My family is Catholic, not me, not anymore after…well, just after what I saw it do to someone I care about. Consider me an agnostic, but really, I don't have a religion anymore.

"Captain Spiegel said we should make our own rules. I'll steal a line from Groucho Marks and say, "Hooray for Captain Spiegel."

"You once told me you were honored to be my wingman. Well, I feel the same way about being yours, and I plan to be your wingman for the rest of my life."

Matt said, "I want you to have a normal life, to get married, and have children. You're the only one of us that can have children. You'd be a great dad."

Jeff said, "Not now, maybe later, years from now, who knows. But before you send me off to the stud farm, I want to spend some time with you, just you, until you get sick of me without anyone firing at us."

Matt said, "I don't think I'll ever have the strength to let you go again."

An exasperated Jeff said, "Good, finally!" then added, wearing a lecherous smile, " Now, how long do we have until sunrise and someone on shore could see us?"

Matt, grinning, said, "You do know there's a cabin below with a bed and heater, right?"

THE END

Thank you for taking the time to read "Mustang Wingman." Please take a moment to rate and review the book; your interest and feedback are greatly appreciated.

Thomas Willard © 2021

The story continues with "Sabre Wingman," book #3 in the

Wingman series, available on Amazon at

https://www.amazon.com/dp/B0BM836BSJ

Made in United States
Troutdale, OR
12/27/2023

16424857R00126